Whatever After
ABBY IN WONDERLAND

Read all the Whatever After books!

SPECIAL EDITION

Whatever After

ABBY IN WONDERLAND

SARAH MLYNOWSKI

Scholastic Inc.

Copyright © 2017 by Sarah Mlynowski

This book was originally published in hardcover by Scholastic Press in 2017.

ISBN 978-0-545-74667-0

10 9 8 7 6 5 4 3   18 19 20 21

Printed in the U.S.A.   40

First printing 2017

for my nephews, jack and ryan swidler.
now that i've dedicated a book to you, will you
finally follow me on instagram?

chapter one

Just the Four of Us

*t*he good news: There's no school today, even though it's a weekday. YAY! It's one of those "Teacher Days" where all the teachers go in and have boring meetings but we kids get a day off.

The better news: I'm spending the entire day with my best friends, Frankie and Robin.

The terrible news: WHERE we are spending the day. Guess whose house we're going to? No, not Frankie's. Nope, not Robin's, either. And not mine. Give up?

We're going to Penny's house. Yes, Penny. THAT Penny. As in, Robin's other best friend. The one who is always trying to steal Robin away from me.

My parents are driving me to Penny's right now. My mom and dad both have work today — they're lawyers and they need to be in court. Frankie and Robin's parents both work, too. So Penny's mom — who knows my mom from some school committee they're both on — invited Robin, Frankie, and me over to *their* house.

Great.

"We're here," Dad announces as my mom turns our car into Penny's driveway. My stomach flip-flops and I frown.

"Whoa!" my little brother, Jonah, says, glancing out the window of our car. "Penny lives in a *castle*?"

"It's a mansion," I say, staring at the huge stone house and sitting up straighter. It *does* kind of look like a castle. Humph.

I knew that Penny lived in a ginormous house, but I've never seen it before. Penny and I aren't exactly friends.

"Hey," Jonah whispers to me. "Doesn't it look just like the castle from *Aladdin*? Remember, the one that the evil genie tried to steal and —"

I narrow my eyes at my brother and nudge him in the ribs with my elbow. "Shush!" I whisper. "Not in front of Mom and Dad."

My parents DO NOT know that Jonah and I visit fairy tales. But we really do. Pinky swear.

When we moved into our house in Smithville, Jonah and I found a magic mirror in the basement. The mirror is bolted to the wall, and it has this beautiful carved stone frame that's decorated with small fairies. Jonah and I discovered that if we knock on the mirror three times at midnight, a nice fairy named Maryrose, who lives in the mirror, will make the glass turn purple and swirl. Then Jonah and I can step through the glass and straight into a fairy tale. We've been to a ton of different ones, including *Cinderella, Sleeping Beauty, Beauty and the Beast, Hansel and Gretel*, and yep, *Aladdin*. Jonah and I always mess up the stories — sometimes by accident, sometimes on purpose. But it usually works out for the best.

Usually.

I put my hand in my sweatshirt pocket and touch the tiny piece of stone in there. Last night, after dinner, I was down in the basement, playing with our dog, Prince. Jonah and I often take

Prince along into the fairy tales. (We actually *found* him in a fairy tale, but that's a whole other story.) It was only eight P.M., so I knew Maryrose wouldn't let us through the mirror. But dogs can't tell time. Prince kept butting his furry little head against the mirror, probably hoping it would turn purple and start to swirl. The glass didn't swirl, but a *teeny* piece of the stone frame — half a fairy wand — broke off and fell on the floor. I immediately picked it up and hurried upstairs to look for some superglue. But I couldn't find any in my room, and then my parents said it was bedtime. So I've decided to carry the frame piece around with me until I have a chance to fix it. I can't risk the piece — a piece of magic! — getting thrown out by accident. Who knows what problems *that* would cause?

Also, I kind of love walking around with something magical. It's like having a Hershey's Kiss in your pocket, but even better. And less melty.

Although Hershey's Kisses are pretty awesome, too.

"Oops, sorry I said that," Jonah whispers back. He glances toward the front of the car, but luckily, my parents haven't heard anything.

"It's okay," I tell him, ruffling his brown hair.

4

Jonah is going to spend the day at his friend Isaac's house. Maybe I should ask to go to Isaac's, too. At least then I won't have to deal with Penny.

Nah. Penny plus Robin plus Frankie is still better than two seven-year-old hooligans playing Dinosaur War, which is a game they recently invented.

"Okay, Abby," Mom says as I unbuckle my seat belt, "we'll pick you up at five thirty tonight."

"Thanks," I say. "Bye, Mom. Bye, Dad. Bye, Jonah."

Jonah is so busy playing with the two miniature dinosaurs in his hands that he barely looks up. "See ya! Have fun at the castle! Watch out for the moat!"

"There's no moat, Jonah," I say. And this definitely will NOT be fun.

I get out of the car and walk to the front door, which is shiny black. There's a huge brass knocker with a lion's head on it, but I can't reach it. I ring the doorbell and hear three melodic chimes from inside.

A woman with short dark hair answers the door. She looks too young to be Penny's mom. She gives me a tight smile. "Hello. You must be . . . I'm sorry, what was your name again?"

"Abby," I say.

"Ah, yes. Abby. You're the last one. Come on in. I'm Sheila, Penny's nanny."

Oh. I didn't know Penny had a nanny.

"Is Abby *finally* here?" I hear Penny snarl. She's standing on the other side of the foyer with her hands on her hips.

I'm not *that* late.

"Hi, Abby," Frankie says softly, looking relieved. She pushes her red-framed eyeglasses up on her nose as she walks toward me.

"Am I that late?" I whisper to her.

"I've been here for about half an hour," she whispers back, biting her thumbnail. "I was the first to arrive. Robin just got here."

Yikes. Poor Frankie. She's not exactly friends with Penny, either.

"Isn't Penny's house AMAZING?" Robin asks, twirling around.

It is kind of amazing. The floor is marble. There's a sweeping staircase. And a golden chandelier wider than the four of us combined dangles above my head.

But mostly I'm distracted by Robin and Penny's outfits. They're both wearing jeans and orange long-sleeved shirts. Penny's blond hair is in a super-high ponytail, held in place by a purple elastic. Robin's curly reddish hair is in a super-high ponytail, also held in place by a purple elastic. They are clearly matching on purpose because there's no way that they'd happen to both be wearing that. Penny loves to match with Robin. It's super annoying. Penny also loves to tell Robin — and everyone — what to do. It's *extra* super annoying.

I glance at Frankie, who's wearing a cute red T-shirt with black leggings. Her straight dark hair is loose and falling in front of her face, like she's hiding behind it. Frankie can be a little shy. I'm sure she was not thrilled to be alone with Penny earlier.

My curly brown hair is also loose, and I'm wearing my blue hoodie and jeans. Frankie and I clearly did *not* get the orange-shirt-and-ponytail memo.

But at least Frankie, Robin, and I all have on our FRA necklaces. They're these beaded necklaces with the initials of our first names: Frankie-Robin-Abby. Penny doesn't have one.

"Guess what," I hear Penny saying. "My mom said I could invite a friend to my next horseback riding lesson and Robin is so excited that she gets to come. She's never been on a horse! Can you believe that?"

"A lot of people haven't been horseback riding," I say, although I have. Only in fairy tales, though, so I can't exactly give that as an example.

"Well, girls," Sheila the nanny says. "I'm going to start cooking. I have a special feast planned for you for lunch. Spaghetti with tomato sauce and garlic bread."

"Yum," Robin and I say at the same time.

Penny frowns and links her arm through Robin's. Penny does not like when Robin and I match.

"Don't get too excited," Penny snaps. "Sheila is not the world's best cook." I look over to see if Sheila heard this, but, thankfully, she's on her way to the kitchen. "My last nanny, Maggie, was a million times better," Penny goes on. "She was the coolest. But my mom caught her trying on her designer dresses, so she got fired."

"Oh, no," Frankie says, her jaw dropping. "Poor Maggie!"

"Poor *my mom*," Penny says. "I wouldn't want someone trying on my clothes. Would you?" She shudders. "Anyway, Sheila isn't that bad. She lets me watch TV until whatever time I want."

"Are your parents here?" I ask. I assumed Penny's mom would be around, since she set up this play date.

Penny shakes her head. "They're in London. My dad had a meeting and my mom went along. She loves London. It's her favorite city. Mine too. Everyone drives on the wrong side of the street there. It's hilarious. I would have gone with them, but they don't like me to miss so much school."

"So your nanny stays overnight?" Frankie asks.

"Obviously," Penny says. "I bet I could stay by myself, though. I'm really responsible."

Is she joking? "You can't stay by yourself," I scoff. "Ten year olds are not allowed to stay by themselves. It's against the law."

"I'm eleven," Penny says, her eyes narrowing.

"It's still against the law," I say. "Trust me. I know this kind of stuff. My parents are lawyers." I'm going to be a lawyer, too, one day. And then I'm going to be a judge. But first I'm going to be a lawyer because that's the rule. I love rules. And one of them is definitely that eleven year olds are not allowed to stay alone.

"How old do you have to be to stay alone?" Robin asks.

"Oh. Um. Sixteen, I think." Or maybe it's fourteen. I'm not a hundred percent sure. I'm not going to tell them that, though. I just know it's not *eleven*. Obviously.

"I'm so jealous of you, Penny," Robin says, playing with one of her curls. "You don't have any parents here to get on your case! Or annoying big sisters. You basically have your whole house to yourself. You can do whatever you want. My sister never lets me watch what I want to on TV. And I have to go to sleep by nine. You're so lucky."

"Totally," Penny says, looking at me smugly. Then she claps her hands. "Okay, girls, now that Abby is *finally* here, we're going outside to play crazy eights. Then we'll have lunch. Then I want to show you some of my horseback riding videos. You have to see the time I won first place. And second. And first again. Then I want to show you my portfolio."

I'm exhausted already. "Your what?" I ask.

"Don't you know what a portfolio is?" Penny asks, rolling her eyes.

"No," I admit.

"It's all of my artwork. Well, besides that." She points to a painting of a bowl of strawberries that's sitting on a side table. "I'm going to ask my parents to put that one in a frame."

The painting is good. Really good. The strawberries look almost real. I have to admit that Penny's a talented artist. Not that I'd ever admit that to *Penny*. It would only make her more stuck-up.

"And then we'll have a lip-syncing contest," Penny continues. "I picked out the music ahead of time. Come on. Let's go. We're already behind because of Abby." Penny doesn't wait for us to answer. She just grabs Robin's hand and yanks her toward the back door.

"She is so annoying," I mutter to Frankie. "I don't want to watch her horse videos! Why would I want to watch her horse videos? And she already picked out the music? What if we don't like the music? What if we don't *know* the music? How are we supposed to lip-sync if we don't know the music? I can't fake it!"

"You just say 'watermelon,'" Frankie tells me.

"Huh?" I ask.

"If you don't know the words to a song, just say 'watermelon' again and again," Frankie explains, and pushes up her glasses.

I laugh and link my arm through hers. "Where did you learn that?"

"I read it somewhere."

Frankie reads a lot of books. For our school read-a-thon a few months ago, she read twenty books in one month. She practically reads a book a day.

I read a lot, too, but not *that* much. I have other stuff to do. Like homework and dance class and watching TV and fairy tale hopping.

But I definitely read more than Penny. She only read *one* book for the read-a-thon.

"Hurry up, guys!" Penny yells as she steps onto the patio. "You're so slow!"

I grumble something not so nice under my breath.

"What did you say?" Penny asks, glaring at me.

I give her a big, fake smile. "Watermelon," I tell her.

chapter two

Really Crazy Eights

Penny's yard is huge and has a million trees and a big bird-bath fountain without any actual birds in it. Birds can probably sense meanness.

The yard is surrounded by a fence, and on the other side I can see miles of green grass and trees. Penny lives right next to Elm Ridge Golf Club. Not that I've ever been to Elm Ridge Golf Club. My parents don't belong to a golf club. And I've never played golf before. But I *have* played mini golf. I'm pretty good at it, actually. I once got a hole-in-one on the last hole and won a free game.

A gust of wind blows through my hoodie. "It's kind of cold," I say. "If we have to play cards, maybe we should play inside?"

"No," Penny says. "I want to play outside. It's warm enough and it's not that windy."

It is *so* that windy. But whatever. If the cards start blowing away, I'll get to say I told you so.

I kind of love saying *I told you so*.

We all sit down at the table on the patio and Penny starts dealing the cards. Seven to each of us.

"I play with five each," I say.

"Me too," Frankie adds, blushing.

"I play with seven," Robin says.

Humph. Since when?

Penny shrugs. "Well, it's my house, my rules," she says.

She really is horrible. Why is Robin even friends with her? I don't get it.

"Let me take a selfie of us before we start," Robin says, and pulls out her phone.

Robin is obsessed with her cell phone. She's not allowed to do much with it besides call her family and take pictures, but it never leaves her side. She has a totally jazzed-up fuchsia pink case, too. Robin's one of the only kids in our grade with her own phone. Not even Penny has one yet! No wonder Robin loves it so much.

Robin lifts up the phone and holds it over us. "Smile!" she says.

We smile.

Snap.

"Fab," Robin says.

Then we start the game. Penny flips over the jack of hearts, which means we can either play a jack or a heart or an eight. I have none of those. Great. Just terrific. I reach into the pile of cards and pick up the seven of clubs. Then the ten of diamonds. I pick up another five cards until I finally, finally get a heart. Yes!

Too bad I'm stuck with a million extra cards, though. The goal of the game is to get *rid* of all your cards.

Robin changes the suit to clubs. Frankie has to pick up a few cards, but then she plays the six of clubs, and then Penny plays the six of hearts, which means I have to play a heart again.

Argh! I pick up more cards. And more cards. I need a heart!

I can't let Penny beat me after five minutes. I pick up another card. Five of diamonds. Humph.

"Did I tell you guys that I was invited to attend a super-elite art program at the museum downtown?" Penny says, smiling to herself.

I pick up another card. Four of diamonds. Argh.

"I want to do it, but I'm pretty busy with horseback riding," Penny goes on. "Plus, I don't think they're advanced enough for me. I might have to apply to a special program in New York City over the summer. And —"

Is she seriously bragging about herself while we're in the middle of a game? I turn over another card. Seven of clubs.

"— I'm sure I would get in. And I would get to stay in a college dorm! How fun would that be?"

Is she trying to distract me? She is. She so is. I turn over another card. Three of diamonds.

"I have to show you guys the paintings I did of the stable. They're really good."

"Penny!" I yell.

"What?"

"Can you stop?" I say.

Penny's eyes widen in surprise. "Stop what?"

"Talking! You're trying to distract us!"

"I am not," she huffs. "How could I distract you, anyway? All you have to do is pick up a card. There's no *skill* involved."

She has a point. But whatever. "You're making it hard to focus."

Frankie and Robin look at me. Then Penny. Then back at me. It's like they're at a tennis game. I wish one of them would jump in, but I know they won't. Frankie's too timid to get involved and Robin doesn't like to choose sides.

"*Excuuuuse* me." Penny crosses her arms in front of her chest. "I'll stop talking."

"Thank you," I say. I flip over another card. Two of spades. ARGH. Did Penny hide all the hearts on the bottom of the deck?

"Good focusing," she says with a smirk.

I flip over another one. Queen of hearts. Finally! Wahoo! I did it! "There," I say, but just as I'm about to slam the card down in victory, a gust of wind blows it right out of my hand. "Hey!" I cry as I watch the card fly over the patio and onto the grass. "Come back!"

"Just pick another card," Penny barks.

"No way," I say, jumping out of my seat. "It was the queen of hearts. I want *that* card." But the card continues floating away from us like a kite without a string. "I told you it was too windy to play cards!"

"Forget the card, Abby," Penny snaps. "Don't be difficult."

Difficult? Me? I'm the one who's being difficult? I'm not the one being difficult! She is the queen of being difficult! "I'm getting it," I say, and jump down the three steps off the patio.

"I'll help!" Robin cries, and I hear her stomping down the steps behind me.

Hah! She's helping me. Take *that*, Penny. Robin is following me. Not you. Me.

"Where'd it go?" I ask.

"It's right there," Robin says, pointing to the edge of the birdbath fountain.

"Good eye," I say.

I'm about to snatch the card when another gust of wind comes, lifting the card up and sending it soaring right over Penny's white fence, out of the backyard, and straight onto the golf course.

"It's gone!" Penny calls. "Pick another card."

There is no way, no how, no chance I am picking another card. I am getting *that* card. But how?

"Look, Abby," Robin says, and I turn around to see her standing on the edge of the fountain. "The fence isn't that high. We can climb over."

Yes. Yes, yes, yes! I can definitely climb over the fence. I've climbed over a ton of fences before. And yay! Robin's on *my* side. Not Penny's! I step onto the fountain beside Robin.

"What are you doing?" Penny calls nervously from the patio.

"We're going to get the card," I say. "Ready, Rob?"

"Guys, be careful," Frankie warns, biting her thumbnail and standing up from her chair.

"I'm not supposed to go onto the golf course," Penny says.

"You're not going," I say. "We are."

Robin winks. "One. Two. Three!"

We both climb on top of the fence, and then swing our legs over.

"Come back!" Penny hollers from the patio. "Right now!"

"I see it," I say, happily ignoring Penny and pointing to the card on the ground. "I'm going to get it. You can just stay up here and —"

Before I finish my sentence, Robin has already jumped off the fence. "Wahoo!" she screams as she goes.

Okay, then.

I guess I'm going, too. I land on the grass with a thud. Ouch.

I stand up and reach for the card. Another gust of wind blows it out of my hand. Tricky little thing.

"Guys!" Penny cries. I turn to see her and Frankie standing behind us, the gate open behind them.

There was a gate? That would have been slightly easier.

I turn back around. From where we're standing, we can see the entire golf course: short green grass, small hills, and tiny flags.

"There's the card!" Robin cries, pointing. She starts running through the golf course toward one of the flags.

"What if she gets hit by a ball?" Frankie asks.

Penny shakes her head. "No one's golfing right now. The course is closed this month. Too cold."

"I told you it was too cold to be outside!" I can't help but say. "Also too windy."

"It's not that windy," Penny says as the wind blows her blond ponytail straight up in the air.

"Are you kidding me?" I cry.

Robin stops and whirls around. "I don't know where it went!" she calls.

Then I see the card. Just sitting there on the grass, right beside Frankie.

"Grab it, Frankie!" I say.

"'Kay," Frankie says and reaches out. Of course that's exactly when the wind lifts the card off the ground and away from her. Frankie follows the card up a small hill. The card seems to take a flying leap over the hill . . . and then it disappears.

"Wait!" Frankie yells and runs after it. And then Frankie disappears.

"Frankie!" I yell, reaching the top of the hill. I don't see Frankie anywhere on the horizon. Where did she go? What happened?

I take a few steps down and stop right before a massive hole in the ground. It's about four feet across and deep. Very deep. So deep I can't see the bottom.

What I *can* see is Frankie half dangling in the hole, her fingers digging into the ground, trying to keep herself from falling all the way inside.

Oh, no!

"Abby!" Frankie cries, her dark hair billowing behind her, her glasses crooked on her face. "Help me!"

"Oh my goodness!" I say, feeling sick. Why is there a huge hole in the middle of the golf course? Is that where the golf balls go? How does anyone ever get them out?

I reach down and try to grab Frankie's hand and pull her up, but she's too heavy.

"Penny! Robin!" I holler.

They appear by my side, huffing and puffing. When Robin sees Frankie, she lets out a strangled cry.

Penny grabs Frankie's other arm, and Robin holds on to the back of her shirt.

"Come on, guys!" I shout.

"I'm trying!" Penny says.

"I can't hold on!" Robin says.

Frankie is squirming like crazy. "Don't let me fall," she says, sounding panicked. "I don't see a bottom!"

"We won't," I promise. I will not let her fall. I will not. I will NOT.

I lie down flat on my belly to try to get a better grip. But Frankie's still sliding. Now Penny and I are each holding one of Frankie's hands. Robin is still holding her shirt.

"Don't let go," I tell Frankie, my heart racing.

"I'm trying not to, but Penny's hands are all sweaty!" Frankie says.

"*My* hands are sweaty?" Penny yells. "*Your* hands are sweaty!"

"My hands are *definitely* sweaty," Robin says.

"Please save me," Frankie begs.

"WE'RE TRYING TO!" Penny yells.

"We will," I say, but Frankie's sliding farther down. "Can you dig your feet into the sides to give you a better hold?"

She tries to kick her foot to the side, but the swinging motion makes her loosen her grip. The next thing I know, her hands aren't holding our hands anymore. She's not holding us at all. Instead, her arms and legs are spread out and she's screaming — loudly — as she falls down the hole.

"HEEEEELLLLP MEEEE*eeeeeeeeee*," her voice echoes. It gets quieter and quieter the farther she falls.

Until we can't hear anything at all.

chapter three

Down the Rabbit Hole

Oh, no. Oh, no.

Oh, NOOOOoooooo.

Robin, Penny, and I are still staring into the hole, but now there's nothing to hear or see. Just blackness.

We lost Frankie! Where did she go? Where does the hole lead?

Robin gets on her knees and peers in. "I can't see her! How deep can the hole be?"

"I don't know," I say. I shiver, remembering the echoing sound her voice made as she fell. "But I have a bad feeling that it's very, very deep."

And then, as we're gaping at the hole, I notice that it's starting to shrink. To slowly, slowly, close up.

Huh? Why is that happening? That doesn't make any sense! I hate things that make no sense.

"I think we should get my nanny," Penny says, her voice trembling.

My sweatshirt pocket starts to buzz.

I frown. What is that? Did one of my parents' cell phones somehow make its way into my pocket? No, that doesn't seem likely. The buzzing stops. Could it be a bee or a wasp? I carefully feel the outline of the object against my sweatshirt. It's hard. And has jagged edges. And —

Oh! It's the piece of the broken mirror frame from my basement!

The mirror piece starts to buzz again.

Is it trying to tell me something?

The piece of frame starts to shake back and forth. Yes, I'm pretty sure it's trying to tell me something. And I'm pretty sure it's trying to tell me that the massive hole in the ground is somehow related to the magic mirror in my basement.

Wait. Is the hole a portal into a fairy tale? But how can it be?

It's a hole in a golf course! And I usually go into fairy tales with Jonah and Prince. And they're not here. Prince is at home, and Jonah is at Isaac's. I don't go into fairy tales with my friends. I did once, when Robin sleepwalked into the story of *Sleeping Beauty* with me and Jonah. But that was an accident and that was still at my house, at midnight. But if this hole *is* a magic portal, that means Frankie's already inside a fairy tale. Alone. And she doesn't even know that she's in a fairy tale since she's never been in one before. She has no idea what's happening. She's probably still screaming and totally terrified.

The hole keeps slowly shrinking. The portal could close for good any minute.

I have to help her. Now.

My pocket buzzes a third time.

I swallow. Hard. "I need to go in after Frankie," I say.

"No!" Penny says. "That's crazy. Why would we do that? Use your brain, Abby!"

"I am using my brain," I say. "I said *I'll* go after her. You stay here. I'll be back as soon as I can, okay?"

Robin's eyes light up. "I'm coming, too!"

"No, Robin, you should stay here with Penny. I won't be that long. I'll —"

"Geronimooooo!" Robin cries, and the next thing I know, she jumps into the hole like she's jumping off a diving board, her knees pulled in to her stomach.

And down she goes.

"Robin!" Penny cries, but it's too late.

I should have seen that coming. Robin can be a wee bit impulsive.

"I'm going," I say. I take a step forward to jump.

"No," Penny says, grabbing on to my arm. "Let's get Sheila. Or maybe the fire department. They have ladders!"

I shake my head. I don't want any grown-ups knowing what's going on. The fairy tale stuff is supposed to be a secret. "I can find Robin and Frankie. I promise. Just let go of me."

"No! You're not jumping in there!" Penny cries, holding my arm in a death grip. "You are my guest and you're my responsibility! I'm getting help!"

The hole is shrinking faster now. This is bad.

"I can't let you get help," I tell Penny.

"You can't stop me!"

"Oh, yes, I can," I say.

And before she realizes what's going on, I jump inside the hole and yank Penny with me.

Whoooooosh!

"Ahhhhhh!" Penny screams as we fall.

Except we're not really falling. We're kind of gently sinking, like we're in a pool. A pool without water.

It's still dark, but I can see Penny right beside me. Her eyes are shut and her mouth is open and she looks completely freaked out.

"This isn't happening . . . this is NOT happening . . . THIS IS NOT NOT NOT HAPPENING!" Penny cries. Her fingers are spread wide as if she just painted her nails and she's waiting for them to dry.

And wait — there's Robin. She's just a few feet below us!

"Robin!" I call out as we all keep sinking. "You okay?"

"This is amazing!" Robin cries. She does a somersault in midair. "I'm flying! I wish I had a cape!"

"Do you see Frankie?" I ask her.

"No!" she says, and giggles. "But I see a kitchen!"

Huh?

A few seconds later I see it, too. A kitchen. White cupboards swirl near us. Is that a jar of orange marmalade? It is! Then a bookshelf full of books is whooshing through the air beside us. And a chair. Then there's a bed with a flowered quilt. And a loaf of bread.

What in the world is going on?

Okay, this hole *has* to be related to the magic mirror in my basement. I mean, we HAVE to be falling somewhere. Somewhere that will lead to a fairy tale. It's not the way I usually get to fairy tales, but this is clearly magic. The real world does not have flying loaves of bread.

"THIS IS NOT HAPPENINGGGG!" Penny screams again as we all continue to sink-fall.

We pass a polka-dot umbrella. And then a blackboard etched with a tic-tac-toe game. A tray of peanut butter and banana sandwiches. A shelf with a container of baby powder on it.

"I must be dreaming," Penny says, nodding to herself. "Yes. This is a dream. It has to be a dream."

Hmm. If Penny thinks this is a dream, that wouldn't be so

bad. When we get out of here, I can just tell her that she woke up. Then she won't tell anyone about anything strange she saw.

"Yup," I say happily. "It's a dream. A lovely dream!"

"Yes! Robin and I are on an adventure!" Penny says, all three of us still drifting downward. "But why are you in it, Abby? I never dream about *you*."

"Sorry," I say as I duck a flying jar of mayonnaise.

I wish I knew what fairy tale we're in. What story has a flying jar of mayonnaise?

Nope. Can't think of any.

A bottle of ketchup whizzes by my head. Can't think of any story that has those, either.

But, aw, ketchup! Jonah would get a kick out of that one. Jonah loves ketchup. No, Jonah is *obsessed* with ketchup. He puts it on everything. Fries. Mac and cheese. Bread. He would take a bath in ketchup if my parents would let him.

He's going to be so bummed he missed this.

"Do you think we're going to come out on the other side of the world?" Robin asks. "Like in Australia?"

"My parents are taking me to Australia next Christmas," Penny says. "They promised."

We're going to have to land soon. This hole can't go on forever, right?

And just like that . . .

BOOM!

We land hard. The floor is wood, and feels bumpy like a tree trunk. Ouch. I rub my legs as I scramble up. I need to get my bearings.

We're in a long hallway and it's hot in here. The ceiling is a banana yellow and the walls are made of black and white tiles, like a chessboard. Except there's no pattern. It's just uneven patches of black and white.

Penny grabs my leg, then my waist, then my shoulders as she pulls herself up. "What a weird dream," she says.

"I don't know about you guys, but I'm wide awake," Robin says cheerfully. "And this is fab."

"No. It's a dream," Penny says. "It has to be. This is all in my imagination."

"It is," I say, nodding. "It's all in your imagination." I need her to believe that. It will make everything so much easier.

"I don't think it is," Robin says, shrugging. "Sorry, guys. It's real."

Penny crosses her arms in front of her. "It's a dream!"

"Yeah," I say. "It's totally a dream." *C'mon, Robin, quit blowing my cover!*

"It's not a dream," Robin says. "I'll prove it." She reaches over and pinches Penny hard on the arm.

"Hey," Penny cries. "That hurt!"

Then Robin reaches over and pinches my arm, too.

"Ouch!" I say, rubbing the red spot she left.

"See? If it hurts, you're not dreaming. Told you."

"Does that even really work?" I grumble. "Seems bogus to me."

"But . . . but . . . but . . ." Penny's eyes widen again and take in the black-and-white walls. "This is real?"

"No," I insist.

"Yes," Robin says.

"This is REAL?" she asks again. "It can't be." Penny pinches her own arm. "Ouch! No! Impossible!" She pinches herself again. "Ouch! No! Still impossible! Tell me the truth! TELL ME THE TRUTH!"

"Fine. It's real," I admit. I'll have to come up with another explanation for all this later anyway.

"But how?" Penny cries. "And why? I want to go home!" She looks up toward the hole, which has now closed above us. "How do we get out of here?"

"I'm not exactly sure yet, but it's going to be okay," I say, since she seems totally panicked.

"How could it possibly be okay?" she asks. "We're stuck underground! And look at us! We're covered in dirt! I've never felt more disgusting in my entire life! This is all your fault, Abby. Why did you go onto the golf course?"

I'm about to snap back at her when I remember — Frankie.

Oh, no. Where is she?

"Frankie! Frankie? Are you here?" I call out. I wait for her to answer. And wait. Nothing.

"I can't believe she fell in here," Penny grumbles. "What a klutz."

"Hey," Robin says softly. "Don't be mean. It was an accident."

Penny flushes. "She fell in by accident, but *you* jumped in." Then she turns to me. "And you pulled *me* in!"

Now I kind of wish I *had* left her behind. I finally, finally get to go into a fairy tale with friends, and I bring Penny? Annoying, show-offy, Robin-hogging Penny? What's wrong with me?

Penny cranes her neck to see the end of the hallway. "Maybe there's another way out. This place is so bizarre. Yes. Look! There's a door."

Up ahead there *is* a door. A blue door. No, wait. There are a lot of blue doors. Like fifty or so. I walk over and try to open one, but it's jammed. Locked probably. Penny tries another door and it's also locked. Robin runs down the hall and tries some others. We all run from door to door, trying every one, calling out to Frankie as we go.

There's no answer from Frankie. And not one door opens. What fairy tale has a lot of doors? Where *are* we?

"There's one more," Robin says, pointing to the last blue door at the end of the hall.

I almost missed it, because it's so small. Like a dog door but even smaller. It has a key in it. I turn the key and the door opens. Wahoo! But it's such a small door that I can't fit more than my face through it. I lie flat on the floor on my stomach to get a better look. It's not like my clothes can get any dirtier, as Penny has already pointed out.

Whoa.

I can see a beautiful green garden outside.

"There's a garden," I say.

Penny rolls me out of the way. "Let me see," she demands, peeking through the tiny door. "Ooh. Abby's right. We have to go outside!"

"The door is way too small to get through," I say. I stand up and dust off my jeans. Then I notice a glass table behind us. A glass table that was not there before. "Um, guys? Was that table there a second ago?"

"I don't know . . ." Robin says, her brow furrowed. "I don't think so? But it must have been?"

We hurry over to the table. On it is a small bottle, half-filled with amber-colored liquid. Next to the bottle is a Post-it note that reads: DRINK ME.

Drink me?

Wait a minute. Falling down a hole . . . a hallway with doors . . . a garden outside . . . a key . . . Drink Me . . .

This all feels so familiar. I rack my brain to try and remember. I should know most fairy tales by now. My nana read them all to me back when we lived in Chicago. And since then, I've reread all the fairy tales that my school library has. That way I'll be prepared for anywhere that Maryrose sends us.

But I can't seem to place this one . . .

Robin scrunches up her face. "Where have I seen that 'Drink Me' note before? I know I've seen it somewhere."

"Of course you've seen it," Penny says, shaking her head. "It's from *Alice's Adventures in Wonderland*!"

Oh.

OH.

The hole we fell down.

The hallway with locked doors.

The garden outside.

The potion that says DRINK ME.

Oh. My. Goodness.

We're in *Alice in Wonderland*!

chapter four

Some Kind of Wonderful

O MG!" Robin says, her eyes the size of teacups. "You're
right! Are we, like, INSIDE *Alice in Wonderland*? How
cool would that be? So cool! No, that's impossible. Isn't it? Maybe
it isn't. Stuff like this happens in movies all the time, right? I have
to take a picture!" Robin pulls out her cell phone and aims it at
the table.

Ahhh! What do I do now? Do I tell them the truth? How can
I? I'm not supposed to tell anyone! But now I have to admit it,
don't I? I look from Robin to Penny. Do I have to explain the

whole story? Do I have to tell them about my magic mirror and Maryrose and everything?

I can't let Robin take pictures, can I? But how do I stop her?

Snap. Snap. Snap, goes Robin's phone.

I gaze around the hallway. *Alice in Wonderland*? Could it really be?

I know that *Alice in Wonderland* is the name of the movie. *Alice's Adventures in Wonderland*, as Penny called it, is the title of the book. But does that mean I'm in a novel? Sure, it's old — I think it was written almost two hundred years ago — but it's still NOT a fairy tale. I only fall into fairy tales. Fairy tales don't even have real writers. Yes, the Grimm brothers and Hans Christian Andersen wrote the stories down and published them in books, but no one knows where the *original* fairy tales actually came from.

Alice's Adventures in Wonderland came from an author's mind. Larry Carlton. No. Larry Carroll. No. Lewis Carroll! That's it.

"You're bonkers," Penny snorts. "We're in Smithville, just really far down in the ground. We didn't fall into a story. Wherever we are just has some similarities with the book. People don't fall into stories. And, Robin, if you brought your phone, can you please stop taking pictures and call someone to come get us?"

"Oh," Robin says, flushing. "Right." She looks at her phone. "No signal. Sorry."

Penny balls her hands into fists. "Great. Just great."

"You know what, Penny? You're being kind of mean today," Robin says.

Today? TODAY? But still. Maybe Robin is finally realizing how awful Penny is. Hallelujah!

"I'm not being mean," Penny snaps. "I want to get out of here!"

"But how cool would it be?" Robin asks wistfully. "If we really fell into a movie?"

"It was a book before it was a movie," I say.

"We didn't fall into a book *or* a movie!" Penny cries, crossing her arms tightly. "That's insane! And that book is insane. Have you even read it? The pictures are pretty, but the story doesn't make any sense."

"Wait," I say. "How do you know that the book doesn't make any sense? You're not a reader. You only read one book for the school read-a-thon."

Penny tugs at the base of her ponytail. "I know. And it was *Alice's Adventures in Wonderland*."

"Seriously?" I ask.

She squares her shoulders. "Yes. I have an old copy in my room, so I decided I might as well look at it. It's all bound in leather and has silver-edged pages. An original, maybe? My grandmother got it for me for my eighth birthday. Have you guys read it?"

"I've seen all the movies," Robin says. "I love them! And the teacup ride is my favorite ride at Disney World. I love tea parties. When I was little, I had tea parties all the time. I've never read the book, though. Have you, Abby?"

"Of course I read it," I say quickly. Except not really. I have a copy on my bookshelf, too, and I tried to read it once, but the story is, um, kind of confusing. And I tried to watch the older movie once. But it was really scary. So I turned it off.

This is totally unfair. I *would* have read the book if I thought there was a possibility that I could fall into it. But I've never fallen into a book before. Only fairy tales.

Now what am I going to do? When I fall into a fairy tale, I've read the story. So even though my brother and I mess things up, at least I always know what's supposed to happen.

I feel a pang in my stomach. Oh, Jonah. I miss Jonah. We

always go into fairy tales together. Can I do this without him? Can I do this *with* Penny and Robin? What am I even supposed to *do*? Maryrose must have sent me here, right? But why?

And where's Frankie? I need to find Frankie! I can't let her wander around the story by herself. She's shy! What if she's hiding somewhere, crying?

And what happens next? I don't know because I've never read the book!

ARGH.

Robin has seen the movies. So she knows some of the details. But the movies are usually different from the actual stories.

But Penny read the book. She knows what happens in it.

I shiver. No. I can't do it. I. Can't. Do. It. I can't admit to Penny that I don't know the story. I can't ask Penny for help.

Maybe I can cobble the story together from pieces I've picked up over the years. Hmm. There was definitely something about a tea party and a mean Queen of Hearts. Other than that . . .

Crumbs. I need to know the story.

I clear my throat. "Penny, I think it would be helpful if we review what happens in *Alice's Adventures in Wonderland*."

41

"Why?" she asks. "It's not like we're *really* in a story."

"I know. But just in case someone . . . designed this room to look like the one in *Alice*. Or something. We should know what happens. So we can find Frankie."

"C'mon, Penny," Robin says. "Tell us the real story."

Penny raises an eyebrow. "But Abby knows the story. She says she read it."

My cheeks heat up. "Right. Except . . . I . . . I . . . I forgot it."

"You forgot it?" Penny asks, smirking. "How?"

"I don't know. I just did. Can you tell us the story or not?"

"I'll tell you the story." She puts her hands on her hips. "If you admit you never read it."

Ahhhh. What am I supposed to do here? I need to know the story. "Fine, okay? I never read it."

Robin's eyes widen. "But why did you say you did?"

My tongue gets all tied up. "Because . . . because . . ."

"Because she's a show-off," Penny declares.

"Sorry," I say, looking at the floor. I guess I *was* showing off a little. Or at least, I didn't want Penny to look smarter than me. I glance back up at Penny. "Happy?"

"Very." Penny smirks. "Now. There's this girl named Alice. She's sitting outside with her sister. They're reading a book but Alice is bored. Which I totally understand, since most books, including this book, are boring."

I roll my eyes. I can't believe *Penny* read the book and I didn't. I really can't.

"And then?" I ask.

"Alice sees a talking white rabbit that says something about being late and, for some reason, Alice thinks it's a good idea to follow him right down a rabbit hole."

"She falls down a hole! Just like we did," Robin says. "Oh wow oh wow oh wow. We're really in *Alice in Wonderland*! This is the coolest thing to have ever happened to me!"

I love how excited Robin is. She's the best. I wish she could come into every story with me.

"But *we* didn't follow a talking rabbit," Penny says. "We followed a talking crazy person named Abby."

"Oh, for Pete's sake. You're the one who wanted to play outside!" I holler.

"Do not blame me for this!" she hollers back.

"Guys," Robin says, putting her hands up. "Stop fighting!"

"Can you go on with the story?" I mutter.

"Fine," Penny says, twirling her super-blond ponytail. "So. Where was I? Oh. Right. Alice landed in a weird hallway. There were lots of locked doors and yada, yada, yada, she saw a pretty garden."

"Like that one," Robin says, pointing to the tiny doorway.

"Yeah," Penny says. "And she also saw a key on a table and a note that said 'Drink Me.'"

"See?" Robin says. "That story sounds just like our story!"

"Yeah," I say. "Except we didn't find the key on the table. It was in the door."

"But maybe that's because Alice was already here and used the key to open the door," Robin says.

"There is no real Alice," Penny says. "We're not *really* in a book."

"Then how do you explain the flying mayonnaise? And the fall down the hole?" Robin asks.

"I don't know," Penny says tightly. "There must be some logical explanation."

"Yes," Robin says. "The logical explanation is that we're in *Alice in Wonderland*. And Alice used the key to open the door."

Robin is totally right.

Penny rolls her eyes again. "But Alice never uses the key. She drinks the potion and it shrinks her down and she forgets the key on the table. She doesn't go into the garden until much later in the story. So your explanation makes no sense."

Oh.

"But if it wasn't Alice who used the key . . ." Robin says. "Wait. It was Frankie!"

"You think Frankie drank the potion?" I ask. Is she that brave?

"Yes! She for sure read the book," Robin says. "She would have known to drink the potion so she'd shrink down, and she used the key to open the door."

"Then she's probably in the garden right now!" I say, trying to peer out the tiny doorway.

"Let's go get her," Robin says, reaching for the little bottle on the table. "We'll drink the potion so we can shrink down, too!"

"Guys!" Penny says. "We're not in *Alice in Wonderland*! And there is no way I'm drinking from some random bottle of who-knows-what. It could be poison."

I see Penny's point. If I were here with Jonah, I would NOT let him drink the potion. But if we don't do anything, we'll never find Frankie.

I try to think rationally. "Look," I say, pointing to the half-empty bottle. "Frankie obviously drank some of the potion already. And she must be okay, or she wouldn't have been able to open the door. I think we should drink the poison. I mean, potion."

"You're both nuts," Penny says.

"Okay," I say. "How about one of us tries a TINY sip first? And if that person shrinks, then the rest of us drink it, too. Deal?"

"Deal," Robin says.

Penny rolls her eyes. "Okay. If it shrinks you instead of poisoning you, I'll taste it."

"Fab!" Robin says, and without even hesitating, she picks up the bottle and takes a sip.

"Robin!" I say. "I was supposed to try it first!"

"Sorry. I got excited. But it's not working," she says, putting the bottle back on the table.

"Hmm," I say. "Maybe it takes a few seconds?"

Robin squeals.

"What?" Penny and I ask at the same time.

"I . . . I . . ." Robin's face pinches together. And I realize —
she's shrinking! Oh my goodness. She's like a balloon that's
losing air. I watch in disbelief as my friend gets smaller and
smaller. Her arms are flailing. She's three feet. Two feet. Is she
ever going to stop? What if she disappears?

Finally, the shrinking comes to an end. My best friend Robin
is now about the size of a pencil. Her hands are the size of eras-
ers. She's a miniature Robin, with a tiny reddish ponytail, a tiny
orange shirt, tiny blue jeans, tiny sneakers, a tiny FRA necklace,
and teeny, tiny freckles.

THIS IS SO WEIRD.

Robin screams. It's a super high-pitched scream like she just
inhaled helium.

"Robin is tiny!" Penny shrieks.

"Teeny tiny!" I add.

Penny shakes her head back and forth and back and forth.
"IT WORKED. IT'S REALLY A SHRINKING POTION.
Ahhhh! Does that mean . . . does that mean we're really in *Alice's
Adventures in Wonderland*? We're really IN a book?"

"Seems that way," I say. I can hardly believe it, either. Even after all my fairy tale experience.

I look down at my minuscule friend. "Are you okay, Robin?" I ask.

"I'm better than okay," Tiny Robin chirps. "I'm terrific. That was the coolest thing ever! I'm itty-bitty! Woo-hoo! The potion was real!"

I laugh. Magic is amazing.

"I just can't believe it," Penny says. She kneels down to examine the newly pencil-sized Robin.

I eye the bottle. "What does it taste like?" I ask.

"Like Orange Crush," Tiny Robin replies. "Fizzy but fruity."

"Are we really going to drink it?" Penny asks, standing back up. "Maybe we shouldn't. Who knows what can happen?"

"We're going to get small," I say. I *am* a little nervous. I've turned into a beast and a mouse, flown on a magic carpet, and breathed underwater, among other things. But I've never been tiny.

"Just drink the potion already!" Tiny Robin cries. "C'mon, guys! Turn small and we'll go into the garden to look for Frankie.

And then we can go to the tea party, too. All those little finger sandwiches. Delish!"

My stomach growls. I am hungry. We never did get to have the spaghetti that Penny's nanny was making.

"Do you want me to go first?" I ask Penny.

Penny bites her lip. "*A* does come before *P* alphabetically."

I never realized Penny was so . . . wimpy. Maybe she's just freaked out. I would be, too, if I had never traveled to fairy tale realms.

"Okay," I say. "Here goes nothing." I lift up the bottle and sniff it — and wrinkle my nose. It smells gross. I take a sip. Blech. Orange soda? More like a dirt-and-leaf smoothie.

I quickly swallow some of it down. And wait.

And . . . hey! I'm shriiiiinnnnkkking! My legs are getting shorter. And now my arms. My body is going down, down, down. Now my head and neck are following. The rest of the world is getting bigger as I get smaller.

Eeeeep!

Then the shrinking stops. I stare down at myself. I'm pencil–sized. So are my clothes.

I have to admit, shrinking *was* cool.

"Welcome!" Tiny Robin cries, giving me a tiny high five. We're exactly the same size now. Does that make me Tiny Abby?

The hallway around us looks huge. The glass table looks massive. And Penny looks like a giant.

Ahhhh! Giant Penny! She could squash me with her sneaker in one giant step.

"I'm not sure I want to do this," Penny says, her giant hands shaking.

"Penny, you promised," Robin says. "We have to find Frankie!"

"You don't have to shrink," I say quickly. "You can stay here and wait for us to come back." To be honest, I'd much rather be on this adventure with just Robin.

Penny narrows her eyes, apparently reading my mind. "Sure. And let you have all the fun with Robin without me? I don't think so."

I watch her take a sip of the potion.

In seconds, she's shrinking down, down, down, until she's pencil-sized like us.

Tiny Penny looks down at herself and shrieks. Then she squares her shoulder and lifts her chin. "Ready," she declares.

Robin pushes open the door to outside. She runs out first. I go next, and I fit through easily. Penny follows me out, and the door slams shut behind us.

We're in the garden.

chapter five

A Game of Croquet

W ow!" Robin says. "This is the most beautiful garden I've ever seen!"

It's true. The garden is bright green and carefully tended. There are brick paths lined with red roses, and little white benches to sit on. The hedges are in amazing shapes, like boats and animals. The entire garden smells of freshly mowed grass and sweet flowers. I feel like we're in a dollhouse, or a doll garden. Everything around us is our size. Tiny.

You know who would LOVE this garden? My dog, Prince.

He'd be chasing after butterflies and sniffing the tree roots. And eating stuff.

He really likes to eat flowers. The neighbors aren't his biggest fans.

Maybe it's better that he's not here.

I look up at the sky. It's light blue, and filled with dancing fluffy clouds. Seriously. The clouds are dancing. A pair of clouds shaped like fluffy people are doing what I think is the waltz.

In the distance, I see what looks like a castle. It has turrets and everything. The only weird thing — the castle is all red. "Amazing," I murmur.

"The garden is *okay*," Penny scoffs. "The garden at my summer house is pretty great, too."

Of course she has a summer house.

Robin is running from flower to flower, sniffing each one. "This is so fab. I can't wait to go to the tea party! And to meet the Mad Hatter. And the queen! And Alice! Do you think we'll get to meet Alice? Oh my goodness, we might get to meet Alice!"

"That's true," I say. It *would* be cool to meet Alice. I'm not sure I want to meet the queen, though. Isn't she supposed to be evil? Anyway, we need to focus on Frankie.

I wish I knew what time it is in Smithville. I usually wear my watch when I go into a story, since it keeps track of time back home. But I didn't put on my watch this morning. And if I'm not back by five thirty when my mom comes to pick me up, my parents are going to freak out. And so will Robin's parents. And Frankie's. And Penny's nanny.

Crumbs. I need a watch!

Then I remember.

"Robin!" I call. "What time does your phone say?"

She takes it out of her pocket. "It says . . . six o'clock? Is that possible?"

"I don't think so," I say. "It might have gotten messed up in the fall."

"Or maybe there's a time difference here," she says. "My phone always changes to the local time."

Right. It could be six o'clock in Wonderland.

I look around the garden but don't see anyone. I wonder why we're even here. When Maryrose sends me and Jonah into a fairy tale, she always has a reason. Not that we find out the reason ahead of time — or sometimes ever.

I'm getting a bad feeling. I can't explain it. Yeah, the garden LOOKS pretty. But there's something . . . *off* about it at the same time.

I just want to find Frankie and go home.

"Guys, look!" Robin says, her face all lit up.

I glance over at where she's pointing. Cards? Cards! Like the ones we used to play crazy eights. Except these cards are *walking* around. They are two-dimensional and made out of shiny cardboard, and they have heads. And arms. And legs.

And we're the same size as them. They're human-sized! Oops, no. We shrank, so actually we're card-sized.

Three card-people are standing near us. I can see the little black leaf in each of the four corners of their card bodies. So they're spades. Are they holding paintbrushes? I squint to see better. They are! And one of them is holding a can of red paint.

Off to the side, I see another card — the Two of Spades — biting the nails on his left hand. He's also holding a paintbrush, but he looks worried about something.

Penny, Robin, and I tiptoe closer. We're behind a big red rosebush. The spades are standing on a path edged with perfect white rosebushes. And they're TALKING.

"The Two of Spades is in BIG trouble," the Three of Spades says. He dips the paintbrush into the paint can. He then brushes red paint over a white rose. Then another.

"REALLY big trouble," the Five of Spades agrees. He also dips his paintbrush in the can of red paint and starts painting a white rose red.

"He's gonna lose his head for sure," the Seven of Spades says. He's holding two paintbrushes and paints two white roses red at once.

"Unless we finish in time," Two says, rushing over to dip his paintbrush into the can Five is holding. He starts painting roses very quickly. I can see he's missed a petal.

"Well, don't be sloppy about it, Two!" Five warns. "Or the queen will know! And we'll get beheaded!"

I cringe. "Beheaded?" I whisper. "Seriously?"

Robin cringes, too.

Penny nods grimly. "This queen is not messing around," she says. "She's mean."

Shivers run down my back. "Then we have to get out of here — pronto. We need to find Frankie. Where could she be?" I hope she's okay. Even if she knows the story, she's probably still completely scared.

"Does she play croquet?" Penny asks.

"Huh?"

"There's a croquet court over there." She points ahead to a manicured green lawn. I can make out a white stake in the middle of the grass, and more card-people milling around, holding sticks.

I've seen croquet on TV a few times before my dad switched the channel. It's kind of like mini golf. You knock the ball through an arch instead of hitting it into a hole. And you use a wooden mallet — a stick with a rounded end — instead of a golf club.

"I don't think Frankie plays croquet," I say. I've never played croquet. And Frankie is even less athletic than I am. I'm not sure she's even played mini golf.

"Let's check it out," Robin says excitedly. "I remember the croquet scene from the movie! It's hilarious! Is it the same in the book, Penny?"

"Probably," she says with a shrug. "Okay, let's go."

"If there's no sign of Frankie, though, we have to keep moving," I say.

Robin claps. "Yay!"

It's strange. Traveling into a story with Robin is a little bit like traveling with my brother. She's so excited about everything. Except she's less obsessed with ketchup.

We walk through the garden toward the croquet lawn, passing a couple more card-people. But no one says anything to us or seems to think it's weird that we're here.

Maybe nothing is weird in Wonderland because EVERYTHING is weird in Wonderland?

When we get to the croquet area, I blink. And blink again. Yup, everything IS weird in Wonderland. And what I'm seeing now is the weirdest thing yet.

Instead of holding a wooden club, the Ace of Diamonds is holding a flamingo.

Yes. A real live flamingo. The card-person is playing croquet with a pink bird. At least the flamingo is card-sized, too.

And — I step a bit closer to make sure I'm seeing what I think I'm seeing — the cards are using hedgehogs as BALLS. Yes. Hedgehogs. Those roundish critters with little snouts, black noses, and prickly brownish fur that I've occasionally seen in my yard. These hedgehogs are about the size of my shrunken feet.

I watch the Ace of Diamonds hold the pink flamingo upside down and use its long neck and head as the mallet. He knocks the flamingo against the hedgehog, which goes rolling into . . . into . . .

No. It can't be. But it is! The rectangular goal is not a piece of plastic like I thought. It's another card-person. This one is a Five of Diamonds. And he's bent over sideways to form an arch with his palms and feet. That can't be comfortable.

"Yes!" the Ace of Diamonds cheers. "Score!"

The hedgehog rubs his rear end with his tiny paw and then runs off behind a bush.

"Come back here this instant, hedgehog," the Five of Diamonds, still bent over, demands.

The hedgehog does not come back. But there are many more hedgehogs, all waiting patiently for their turn.

I clear my throat. "Excuse me," I ask the Eight of Diamonds standing nearby. "Have you seen a girl around here? She has dark hair and dark skin and red glasses?"

He shakes his head. "I don't believe I have," he says. "But I am often wrong."

"Hmm," I say. I'm not sure if that's a no or a maybe.

"Would you like to play?" he asks.

"Sure," Penny says just as I say, "No, thank you."

"Come on," Penny says. "We're here anyway. One quick game."

"Yeah!" Robin says. "Maybe the game will lead us to Frankie."

"I don't want to waste time," I say.

"She just doesn't want to lose," Penny mutters.

"Excuse me?" I say, turning toward her.

"You just don't want to lose," she repeats. "I get it. You've never played croquet before. You won't be any good at it. If I were you, I wouldn't want to play, either."

I snort. "Like *you* have played before?"

She flips her ponytail. "Of course I have. I'm quite good."

"Sure you are," I mutter.

"I am!"

"Guys, stop fighting," Robin says. "Let's play!"

"Abby's too scared," Penny says.

"Am not!"

"Are too!"

The steam builds up inside me. "Fine! You want to play? I'm ready!" I march over to where a bunch of flamingos are standing around, stretching their legs. One flamingo huffs when he sees me. I don't blame him. Being a piece of sports equipment does *not* seem like a fun job. I pause.

Without hesitating, Penny reaches under a feathered pink belly and picks up one of the flamingos. She then turns it upside down, but the bird starts flapping its wings. "Stop that, flamingo!" she orders. "You better behave."

The flamingo does not stop flapping.

"Cut. It. Out," Penny says.

She finally gets the bird to stop flapping. But just as she's about to swing the flamingo's head against the hedgehog by its feet, the hedgehog takes off, running in the other direction.

I giggle. What can I say? That was funny.

Penny grumbles to herself. "Okay, big shot. Let's see how you do, Abby."

Oops.

A flamingo walks right up to me. Does this mean he wants to be smacked against a hedgehog? I look at Penny and Robin and shrug. I can do this. How hard can it be? I pick up the flamingo the way Penny did and turn him upside down. I look at the hedgehog by my foot. "Here goes," I say. Maybe if this was how they played croquet on TV, my dad wouldn't switch the channel.

"Wait!" the arched-over card-goal says. "My foot's asleep!" He straightens up and rubs his foot. Then he gets back into position. "Okay, you can go!"

I aim. I shoot.

I totally miss. Both the flamingo and the hedgehog burst into laughter. And so do all the card-people. Great. Just great.

"That was worse than me," Penny says. "Robin, your turn."

Robin's flamingo does as it's supposed to and her hedgehog rolls through the goal!

"Yay, you!" I say.

Robin takes a bow.

"I refuse to not be good at this," Penny snaps, grabbing another flamingo. She aims. She hits. She scores. The hedgehog rolls right into the goal.

So annoying.

"Yessssss!" Penny shouts. "I rule at croquet! Do you think they give out trophies?"

"Don't let the queen hear you say that," the Three of Diamonds warns. "She likes to win."

The thing is, I like to win, too. And I wouldn't mind a trophy. It would look really good in my bedroom. Or maybe I could bring it to school and put it on my desk so Penny has to see it every time she passes me.

I need to try this for real. I pick up another flamingo. I quickly line up my shot and whack the flamingo against the hedgehog. I watch as the hedgehog rolls . . . just to the left of the arched card-goal.

Crumbs.

"Aww, don't feel bad just because *I* scored and *you* didn't, Abby," Penny says, which obviously does make me feel bad.

I shake it off. So what if she's better at weird-croquet? I bet I would be better at it with actual sticks instead of animals. I got a hole-in-one at mini golf! So what if all the other holes took me five tries? Anyway, there are no trophies here. And we really have to go. Why are we even playing this? I put down the flamingo. "This is a waste of time, you guys. We have to focus on finding Frankie."

"If you're sure that's why you want to stop, Abby," Penny singsongs.

"It *is*," I insist. It totally is. It's most of the reason, anyway.

"Thanks for letting us play," Robin says to the Ace of Diamonds.

"Anytime," the card says, and salutes us.

We leave the croquet court and keep walking, scanning the garden for Frankie.

"What is that smell?" Robin asks.

"The smell of flowers?" I ask.

"The smell of losing?" Penny asks.

I roll my eyes.

"It's the smell of dessert!" Robin says. "Oh my goodness. My stomach is growling."

So is mine. Again.

"I'm starving, too," Penny says. "I only had a few potato chips for breakfast and we never got to have the spaghetti Sheila promised us."

"Wait, you had potato chips for breakfast?" I say.

Penny shrugs. "My parents were busy getting ready for their trip."

Sometimes my parents are in a rush in the morning, but we always have breakfast together, even if it's a quick bowl of cereal. Jonah always dribbles milk on his pajamas. I kind of feel bad for Penny. Kind of.

"Hi, girls," a grandfatherly voice says.

We turn around and I gasp. Standing in front of us is a bunny. A white bunny with long white ears. He's wearing a little red coat, silver-rimmed glasses, and a bow tie. There is a large clock dangling from his neck. And he's just our size.

Oh! It's the White Rabbit from the story! Even I recognize him. He's the character who says —

"You're late! You're late! For a very important date!" Robin cries.

Yes. That.

The bunny looks at her strangely. "Riiiiight. I suppose I am. I overheard you saying you were hungry, and I thought I'd point out where you could get some food."

"That's so nice of you," Robin says.

The bunny motions to a long table on the other side of the croquet lawn. "Right there. Do you see? There are a bunch of pies. You are welcome to help yourself to them. I made them."

"Thank you so much!" Robin says. "You're the sweetest."

Penny narrows her eyes. "They're not carrot pies, are they?"

"Carrot pies?" The bunny makes a face. "No! Disgusting! I would never bake a carrot pie. I would never eat a carrot. Carrots are a vile, vile food. I would rather eat dirt than carrots."

Okay, then. I guess contrary to popular thought, not all rabbits like carrots. My cousin doesn't like chocolate. It's incredibly weird, but it happens.

"Thank you," I say. I could eat some pie right about now. Who doesn't like pie? I love all kinds of pie. Chocolate pie. Banana cream pie. Key lime pie. Lemon meringue pie. Mmm.

"Have you seen our friend, by any chance?" Robin asks the bunny. "She's about our height, dark hair, red glasses?"

I flush. I should be thinking about Frankie, not pies.

The bunny nods. "I believe I have."

What? A zing goes down my spine. "You have? Where? Is she okay?"

"I believe she went that way," the bunny says, pointing beyond the table, toward a forest.

"Thank you!" I say. Hurrah! He saw Frankie! That means we're on the right track! We're going to find her! And maybe get pie on the way? "You're the best," I say.

"I am. I really am. Toodles," the bunny says before waving with his tiny bunny hands and hopping off in the other direction.

"Come on," Robin says. "We need energy. Let's have a few bites of the pie and then go rescue Frankie!"

Okay, good. I'm not the only one who could really use some pie.

Robin, Penny, and I hurry over to the table. The pies are tiny — more like tarts. They have fruit on top instead of inside.

"They look delish," Robin says.

Robin and I each pick up one of the tarts. I think they're strawberry. YUM!

Penny does not pick up a tart.

"Penny? Why don't you take one?" I ask.

"They look strange," she says. She crosses her arms over her chest and turns away. "I think I'll pass. I don't normally eat pies baked by small animals."

"Suit yourself. Just don't complain to me that you're hungry later."

"I am kind of hungry," Penny admits. "Fine, I'll try one. But we better not shrink again. Or get poisoned."

"I can't make any promises. But I trust the White Rabbit." I look around for a fork. "Do you see any utensils?"

"Nope," Robin says.

"I guess we have to use our hands," I say.

Penny frowns, picking up a tart for herself. "That's gross. They're in pastry dishes."

"So? Just use your hand as a scooper," I say.

Penny looks horrified.

"Come on," I say. "Follow me."

I stick my hand into the side of the pie and try to edge my fingers underneath. Squishy. Jonah would LOOOOVE this. "See?"

Robin scoops up a big piece.

Penny makes a face, but copies us. "This better be tasty."

"It will be!" I say. "It's strawberry. You like strawberries, don't you?"

She nods.

"Then let's go. One. Two. Three —"

"Wait!" Robin squeals. "Pie pic." She takes out her phone. "It's still six o'clock! The clock must be broken." She snaps a picture of me lifting my hand and carrying a large scoop of tart to my mouth. "Great shot!" she says.

Then she takes a bite and snaps a selfie.

I chew.

Wait a sec.

BLECH. "What's wrong with these strawberries?" I cry, spitting the pie out into my other hand.

"Yuck!" Penny says, scrunching up her face. "Poison!"

"Poison!" I repeat in a scream.

"Guys," Robin says, swallowing. "It's not poison. It's tomato!"

"Oh," I say, feeling silly. A savory pie.

"I'm not having any more," Penny says, spitting the mushed-up tart on the ground. "Forget it."

"It's good," Robin says. "I swear. Try it again."

I take another bite. It's not *that* bad this time, now that I know what it's supposed to be. It's actually pretty tasty. It's just a shock to the system when you expect something and you end up getting something totally different. Like if you think there's milk in your cup, but it's really orange juice. I like orange juice, but I don't want it if I'm expecting milk, you know? Especially if I'm expecting chocolate milk.

"Hey! Hey!" I hear from behind us.

I turn around to see one of the cards waving her hands frantically. It's the Three of Clubs. Her hair is in a long black ponytail, and the bottom of her card is shaped in a skirt.

"What are you doing?" she yells.

She does not look happy to see us.

"Just having some pie," Robin responds, lifting her hand to take another bite.

"Stop that!" the Three of Clubs yells. I spot an *actual* club in her hand. Like the kind of club used to hit people, typically found in caveman cartoons. And she is pointing the club at us. "You are eating the queen's tarts!"

The queen's tarts? Huh?

"These aren't the queen's tarts," I say. "There must be a misunderstanding. These are the rabbit's pies."

"They most certainly are not," the Three of Clubs scoffs.

"They are definitely the queen's. And you ate them! Do you know what she does to thieves? She beheads them!"

"She can't behead me!" Penny whispers. "I have such pretty hair!"

"You are eating the queen's tarts!" the Three of Clubs repeats in a screech.

"But . . . but . . . but . . ." I contemplate denying it, but I'm covered in tart crumbs.

"We'll just explain we only took one bite each," Robin says. "Maybe she'll forgive us —"

Six other card-people appear from behind the Three of Clubs. All of them look angry. All of them are holding clubs in scary positions. Now some of the spade cards are here, too. And they're holding spades. Large metal spades.

"Thieves!" the Five of Clubs shouts as he charges toward us.

"Off with their heads!" yells the Six.

"Penny! Robin!" I whisper-yell. *"Run!"*

chapter six

Here Kitty, Kitty

I'm kind of amazed at how fast the cards can run, considering that they're flat and made of cardboard.

"They look really, really mad," Robin says, her cheeks red from running.

"We can't let them catch us!" Penny cries.

We have to hide! But where?

I look around. There's nothing but rosebushes, grass, benches, hedges, and trees.

"There!" I say, pointing at a ditch covered in ivy.

Robin, Penny, and I go leaping into the ditch and grab the ivy to cover us.

"Where are those terrible thieves?" we hear the girl guard-card ask.

"They probably went that way," another guard-card says.

We hear footsteps pounding away. Phew. "I think they're gone," I say.

"I've never been chased by playing cards," Robin says, out of breath. "How fab was that?"

"Not the slightest bit fab," Penny seethes. "If they catch us, they'll take us before the queen and she'll order our heads chopped off! Didn't you hear them? Heads! Chopped! Off! I like my head just where it is, thank you very much."

Robin rolls her eyes. "You are really grumpy in Wonderland."

Penny frowns.

I've never heard Robin criticize Penny before. I like it.

"I want to go home," Penny says, her voice shaking. "This place is weird. I miss . . . I miss . . ."

I expect her to say her house. Or her parents.

". . . my trophies."

Seriously? "We can't go home without Frankie," I say.

"*You* can't. I can. I'm not even friends with Frankie!"

"But *we* are," I huff. "And I'm not leaving her."

"I'm not leaving her, either," Robin says. She rolls up the sleeves of her orange shirt. "And anyway, why would I want to leave? This place is . . . balloons!"

"It's balloons?" Penny asks. "What does that even mean?"

"It means look!" Robin says, pointing to the sky. "Balloons!"

Sure enough, about a hundred red balloons float by. And then disappear into the clouds. All right, then.

"Balloons," Robin repeats. "Out of nowhere. I love this place. It's fun. No, it's *balloons*."

I laugh. "It really is."

Penny looks at Robin like she's crazy, and then she turns back to me. "How do we know Frankie didn't leave Wonderland already? She doesn't even know we came after her. She could have figured out her way back to Smithville. She's probably back at my house right now, wondering where we are! Meanwhile, I'm worrying about getting my head chopped off."

Penny has a point.

I don't want my head chopped off, either. But I'm not leaving without knowing that Frankie is safe.

And who knows if Frankie can even get back without me? It might be the stone piece of my mirror frame that got us here. It has to be, right?

No matter what, we need to be careful.

When I'm sure the guard-cards are long gone, I get out of the ditch and look around. Robin leaps out, too. Penny stays in the ditch, covered by the long vines of ivy.

I wonder where the rabbit went. And why would he tell us he made the tarts when the queen made them? Was he trying to get us in trouble? And if so, why? Now that I think about it, he did have a strange glint in his eye. Was he lying about seeing Frankie, too?

Penny screams, breaking my train of thought. "Look over there!" she cries. I follow where she's pointing.

Lying down on an incredibly thin tree branch, leaning on one elbow, is a large brown-and-gray-and-white-striped cat.

He's smiling really big and has pointy white teeth.

"He won't bite," I say to Penny. "Don't be such a scaredy-cat." Ha, ha, ha.

Penny shoots darts at me with her eyes.

"The Cheshire Cat!" Robin cries. "It's the Cheshire Cat! I love Wonderland!"

Oh, right. I've definitely heard of the creepy grinning cat.

"He's one of my favorite movie cats!" she adds.

"Who are your other favorites?" I can't help but ask.

"Garfield and the Cat in the Hat. But Cheshire is definitely in my top three. He might be my favorite now that I've met him in person." Robin rushes over to him. "It's so nice to meet you in person! You're my new favorite cat!"

"I know you are, but what am I?" the cat responds.

Robin laughs. "You're the Cheshire Cat!"

The cat keeps smiling. "If you say I am, I must be."

"Great," Penny says, still in the ditch. "A cat who speaks in riddles. Could anything be more annoying?"

Robin rolls her eyes.

Hah!

"Do you like living in Wonderland?" Robin asks the cat.

"Wonderland is where I live and live I like," the cat answers.

Robin nods. "I get it. I totally get it!"

She does? Can she explain it to me?

"Have you seen our friend Frankie?" I ask the cat. "Our age, dark hair, red glasses. She's wearing a red T-shirt?"

"I see everything," he says. "Everything is seen by me."

"Great. So can you tell us where she is?" I ask impatiently.

Penny pulls herself out of the ditch and inspects her jeans for grass stains. "And can you tell us how to get home?"

"You may have fallen through the crack," the cat answers. "But a swallow taken will bring you back."

And then he smiles another TOTALLY CREEPY SMILE and disappears. I shudder. Robin claps her hands in glee.

"Where did he go?" I ask, looking all around.

"That was so cool," Robin says dreamily.

"That was so creepy," Penny says.

I kind of agree with Penny. Not that I'll admit it. "He didn't tell us where Frankie is," I say.

"He told us how to get home, though," Penny says. "So I was right. Frankie must already BE home."

Not if she needs my mirror piece. "But I wonder what he meant," I say. "A swallow taken? Are we supposed to swallow something?"

"Obviously!" Penny says, clucking her tongue. "We have to

swallow something to go home. We put something magical in our mouths. We chew. We swallow. Boom, we go home."

"But what?" I ask. "We've already swallowed two things and they haven't taken us home."

"The shrinking potion and the queen's tarts," Robin says, nodding.

"Right," I say. "So next steps are to find Frankie and also figure out what else in the story there is to swallow." Now it's my turn to swallow. My pride. I have to ask Penny for help. Ugh. I hate asking Penny for help. But I have no other choice. "Penny, I need you to tell us the rest of the story."

"You do, do you?" she asks.

I hang my head in defeat. "I do."

"So once again, you're asking me for help," she says, her voice sounding awfully smug.

"Yes, Penny. Once again I am asking you for help."

"But you forgot to say 'please,'" she says.

"Penny, can you please tell me the rest of the story?" I grumble.

"Sorry, I couldn't hear you. Can you speak up?"

I am going to kill her. I raise my voice. "Please, Penny, pretty please with a cherry on top, can you tell me the rest of the story?"

"You don't have to shout," she says, batting her eyelashes.

"Penny, stop it," Robin says, hands on her hips. "Enough. You have to help us find Frankie."

Penny lowers her eyes. "Sorry," she says, her cheeks bright red. "Um. Well, the thing is . . ."

"Yes?" I say.

She flushes. "I kind of skipped a lot of the book. Since it was so boring."

"You skipped it?" I ask. I don't believe it. "But you won the read-a-thon because of how much money you made for reading that one book!"

"I know I did. I just didn't read every single word. It was super confusing and I had no idea what was going on. I looked at the pictures!"

"But! But!" I cry. "You won the read-a-thon! You're a total scammer!"

Penny crosses her arms. "I am not! I read the first few chapters. I can tell you what happens in those."

"You already told us that," I say angrily. "We need to find Frankie. She probably read the whole thing."

"Everyone calm down," Robin says, hands still on her hips. "Frankie would probably go to the coolest parts of the story, right? And those must be in the movies! The movies wouldn't leave them out."

"I guess," I say. That makes sense. "So what are those?"

"Well, the coolest part of the story includes lots of stuff to swallow," Robin says. "So we should go there. And hopefully kill two birds with one stone."

"Where's there?" I ask, sounding a bit too much like the Cheshire Cat for my liking.

Robin grins. "The Mad Hatter's tea party!"

chapter seven

Bird's-Eye View

You can't just crash a tea party," Penny says as the three of us walk through the forest. She pulls her ponytail tighter. "You need an invitation. My grandmother used to take me to tea at a fancy hotel. We wore frilly dresses and hats."

I glance down at our outfits. Hoodies. Shirts. Jeans. Sneakers. Definitely no fancy dresses or hats.

Robin shrugs. "Oh, don't worry. The rules are different in Wonderland."

"I guess you're right. There don't seem to be any rules in

Wonderland at all." Penny wrinkles her nose. "Does anyone smell that?"

"Smell what?" Robin asks.

Blech. Now I smell it. What is it? I cough and wave the air around my face. It smells like fire. Is something burning? I look around at the trees, but all I see are leaves. Leaves that don't look like leaves. Sure, they're green, but they are shaped like squares.

Yep. Wonderland has square leaves.

"Yuck, is someone smoking?" Penny asks, looking all around. "It smells like my great-uncle's gross tobacco pipe."

"I'll never quit," a scratchy voice says.

Robin, Penny, and I stare at one another. Um, who said that?

"Who are *youuuu*?" the scratchy voice says again.

I look toward where the voice came from. Whoa. No, it can't be.

I see a caterpillar. A long, fuzzy, greenish caterpillar. He's about our size and is perched on top of a giant mushroom. Or maybe it's a normal-sized mushroom since we're all small.

Also, he's smoking a pipe.

"Don't you know that smoking is really bad for you?" Penny asks the caterpillar.

"*Yeeees*," the caterpillar says slowly, and blows letters into the air with the smoke. The letters spell out: B-A-D-F-O-R-M-E.

"Seems he's aware," Penny says, with a cough.

"It's the smoking caterpillar!" Robin gushes. "Yay! I remember him from the movie. I can't *believe* I don't have my autograph book with me. I would get so many cool signatures."

"I'm not sure caterpillars have signatures," Penny says. "Or fingers. He'd better have something for us to swallow."

"We're not going home yet," I say in a rush. "We haven't found Frankie."

Penny raises her nose. "You can stay as long as you'd like. I'm out of here. What can I swallow?"

"In the movies, Alice eats the mushroom and gets bigger," Robin says, pointing to the mushroom cap.

"You'd probably know that if you'd actually read the book," I grumble to Penny.

"You'd probably also know that if *you'd* read the book," Penny snaps back at me.

Fair point.

Penny squares her shoulders. "I'm going to try the mushroom," she says.

"You want to get bigger?" the caterpillar asks. "Why would *youuuu* want to do that?"

"She doesn't want to get bigger," I say. "She just wants to eat your mushroom."

"Oh, *suuuure*," he says, exhaling a trail of smoke. "Use me for my mushroom."

"I'm hoping your mushroom is the swallow that will take me back to Smithville," Penny explains. "And I do want to get bigger, too. I definitely don't want to stay this size forever. I'm taking a bite."

"*Excuuuuuuse* me?" the caterpillar asks, blowing smoke directly in Penny's face. "You need to ask me for my permission first."

"I can't believe I have to ask a caterpillar for *permission* before eating a mushroom," Penny huffs. "This place is bonkers."

"*Yeeees*," he says.

Penny crosses her arms. "Can I take a bite or what?"

"I did not hear a *pleeeease*," the caterpillar says, lifting one of his many hands to his left ear. "Did anyone hear a *pleeeease*?"

"I didn't," I chirp. Serves Penny right after what she put me through before when I asked her to tell me the story. And she didn't even read the whole book! What a liar!

Penny narrows her eyes. "Can I *pleeeeeease* take a bite of your mushroom? Mr. Caterpillar? Sir? Pretty please? With a mushroom on top?"

I will not laugh that she said mushroom on top. I will not. I will just pretend it wasn't funny.

"Sure," he says, blowing smoke directly into our faces. Ugh. I cough. "Go ahead."

Penny tears off a tiny piece of mushroom from the left side. "If I see Frankie back at home, I'll tell her that you're looking for her," she tells me and Robin.

"Gee, thanks," I say.

Penny bites into the mushroom piece, and makes a face as she chews. "This is disgusting."

As the words leave her mouth, I realize that she's getting smaller. And smaller. And smaller. Until she's the size of my leg.

"Crumbs," she says.

Crumbs? That's MY word! Penny just stole my word!

"I didn't go home!" Extra Tiny Penny cries.

"Nope," I say.

"And I'm even smaller than before! How do I get bigger?" she asks the caterpillar.

He blows a smoke circle right at her that is bigger than her entire body. She coughs extra loudly.

"How do I get bigger, please, Mr. Caterpillar, sir?"

"Eat from the right side. It'll make you *biiigger*," he drawls.

Penny jumps on her tiptoes. "Can't reach!"

"I'll get it," I say, snapping a piece of the mushroom off and handing it to her.

"This better work." She pops the piece of mushroom in her mouth like a piece of candy. She chews and swallows. Then she starts growing back to the size she was before. And then she starts growing bigger. And then it's just her neck that's growing. And growing. Oh, wow, she's like a giraffe. Her neck is ginormous.

"Uh-oh," Robin says, peering up past the branches. "I can't even see her head anymore!"

It's true. All we can see is Penny's long, stretched-out neck reaching into the trees.

"Guys!" Penny's voice comes from way above us. "You're not going to believe it!"

"What?" Robin calls.

"You should eat the mushroom!" she calls out.

"But what if we can't shrink back?" I yell up to her.

"The other side will shrink you back," the caterpillar says. "It's not like you're normal-sized now anyway, are *youuuu*?"

Right.

"I can see all of Wonderland!" Giant-Necked Penny shouts. "Come on!"

Robin and I glance at each other, and then we reach for pieces of mushroom from the right side.

I take a small bite.

Yuck. Slimy. It tastes like dirt and —

"Ahhhh!" I shriek as I feel my neck start to stretch like a piece of chewing gum. It's getting longer and longer. Now I can't even see my shoulders. Or my arms or hands. I'm all neck and head.

I try to look out for the branches as my neck races up in the air through the trees, forcing more than one squirrel to leap away. Robin's neck is growing big on the other side of me, and her giant ear almost knocks me into a branch.

Finally, our necks stop growing when we reach Penny. The three of us are right beside one another, all giant heads and SUPER-long necks.

Agh!

"Hi there," Penny says. "You made it. Isn't this incredible?" She slithers her neck through the leaves.

"My neck is so long I can twist around in any direction," Robin cries. "Fab!"

I'm not shocked Robin is having fun, but I can't believe Penny brought us up here. Our heads are stuck in trees! A very angry-looking orange bird with extremely ruffled feathers is glaring at us.

"My neck was perfectly fine down there, attached to my shoulders," I say.

"It's still attached," Penny says.

The bird takes a step closer to us. It looks like a pigeon. An orange one.

"Hello," Penny says cheerfully to the bird.

The pigeon's eyes widen and the next thing I know its beak is poking at my cheek, and the bird is shrieking, "Get lost! Get out of here!"

"Hey! Stop it!" I cry, trying to protect my face with my hands but realizing that my hands are nowhere in sight since they're near the ground with the rest of my body. Instead, I bob my head back and forth, trying to protect myself. She's aiming for my eyes!

"You're the intruder!" the pigeon yells. "You're a snake!"

"Snake?" I repeat. "Why do you think we're snakes?"

"Probably because of our freakishly long necks," Robin says. "Ha! We're not snakes!"

"Then what are you?" the pigeon asks suspiciously.

"We're girls," Penny says.

The pigeon tsks, fluttering her wings. "I don't believe it. I've never seen *girls* that look like you. If you're girls, then where are your arms and legs? Huh? Huh? You're all slithery! You're snakes! You better get out of my nest, you nasty, nasty snakes."

"We are NOT snakes!" I yell as the pigeon aims its beak at my chin. "Stop it!"

"I'm going to get backup," the pigeon says. "Don't you dare go after my eggs. Don't you dare!"

"Terrific," I whine. "Now we have angry birds after us, too."

"I love Angry Birds," Robin says. "Not real ones. Just the game. I wish I could take a picture." I think I feel her hand bump into my hand down below. "Ugh. I can't reach my cell phone."

"Why did you want us to come up here again?" I ask Penny, frustrated. My cheek still hurts from the pigeon's poke.

"I thought you'd want to see."

"I can barely see! The bird tried to attack my eyes!"

"Well, if you could see, you'd see all of Wonderland," Penny says. "And possibly Frankie."

"Oh." I push my head up a bit and take it all in. "Wow."

Wonderland *is* spread out before us. To the right, I see the garden. There's the croquet lawn and the rosebushes and the massive red castle. Straight ahead are rows and rows of houses, all identical and pale pink. To the left are trees with different-colored leaves. All around us are silvery mountains. The strange thing is everything is shimmery. Like it's underwater. Except it's not.

"Too bad we can't see Frankie anywhere," I say, frowning.

Robin is staring at one of the pale pink houses. "Wait. Look in that backyard! I think there are people there. Not card-people but real people. Can you see, can you see? Is Frankie there? Or maybe Alice?"

I squint in that direction. "I can't see that far."

"I have perfect vision," Penny announces, looking over. "And I think it IS Frankie. At least, it's a girl with long dark hair and red glasses."

What? Yes! We found Frankie! Finally! "Is she okay?" I ask Penny frantically. "Does she look freaked out? Is she by herself? Is she hiding somewhere?" I demand.

Penny squints a bit more. "I can't exactly see facial expressions. But she's sitting with other people around a table. The person beside her is" — she squints again — "wearing a big hat?"

"The Mad Hatter!" Robin cries. "Oh, wow, we're going to meet the Mad Hatter! It's the tea party. The Mad Hatter hosts the tea party at his house."

"And there might a rabbit there, too?" Penny goes on, still squinting.

"Is it the rabbit from before?" I ask, annoyed. "The rabbit who told us to eat the pies? I have a bone to pick with him. He better not be trying to pull some trick on Frankie."

"I can't tell if he's the same rabbit," Penny says.

"I thought you had perfect vision," I say.

"It's better than yours," she retorts.

Whatever.

"I've never seen the trees from this angle," Penny continues, looking around. "They're beautiful. I can't wait to paint this when we get home."

Oh.

"Wait, Penny," I say seriously. "You can't tell anyone about this."

She twists her very long neck around to face me. "Why not?"

"Because. We're not supposed to."

She frowns. "Huh? Who says? What are you even talking about?"

I take a deep breath. Should I tell her and Robin? EVERY-THING? About the magic mirror in my basement that sends me into fairy tales? About the fairy named Maryrose trapped in the mirror? About the piece of mirror that's — hopefully — still in my hoodie pocket? I reach my hand over to feel it. Yup. Still there. Phew.

I need Robin and Penny to understand how important it is to

keep our adventure a secret. I take another breath. "Look, I've done this before, okay?" I blurt out. "Well, not this exactly, but I go into fairy tales."

"What?" Penny asks, eyes wide. "You're kidding, right?"

I shake my head.

"I don't believe it," Penny says.

"Believe what you want," I say, crossing my arms. Not that they can see me cross my arms, since my arms are miles below us. But they're crossed.

Robin is staring at me. She opens her mouth and closes it again and then opens it again, looking a bit like a fish. "YOU GET TO DO THIS ALL THE TIME?"

I laugh. "Not *all* the time," I say. "But pretty often. Like every few weeks at least."

"Abby! I can't believe you never told me. You are the luckiest person in the entire world." Robin's head bobs up and down like she's jumping. "Do you always fall into holes?"

"No. I . . . I . . . I . . ." I take a third deep breath. "I have a fairy trapped in my basement mirror. Her name is Maryrose."

Penny snorts.

"I'm serious. I've been going into fairy tales to try and help un-curse her. And I'm the only one who can save her. Well, me and my brother."

Robin's face breaks into a huge grin. "Amazing!" she exclaims.

"That can't be true," Penny says.

"It is," I say.

Robin's eyes light up. "Can I come into the mirror with you?"

I smile. "You did."

Robin's jaw drops and nearly takes off a branch. "I did? NO WAY!"

"Yes! When you slept over." It feels kind of awesome being able to tell her this. "You sleepwalked downstairs and into the mirror. We went into *Sleeping Beauty*. You climbed up the tower, pricked your finger, and fell asleep. When we got back home, you thought the whole thing was a dream."

"I remember that dream!" she says. "It was balloons!"

I laugh. "Are you using that as a word now?"

"I totally am," she says. "So can I go through the mirror with you again?"

"If we ever get home, I'll ask Maryrose," I say. "But you both

94

have to promise not to tell anyone what you saw here. Okay?" I give Penny and Robin serious looks. "Because if people find out, I might not be able to help Maryrose, and then . . . well, she's trapped. Have you ever been trapped?"

"I'm trapped right now," Penny grumbles.

"Right. So you get it. So don't tell anyone. Please."

"We'll see," Penny says, which doesn't make me feel better.

"Can we tell Frankie?" Robin asks.

"When we find her," I start to say, but then —

"Ahhhh!" Penny shrieks.

A flock of angry orange birds, and not the game kind, has landed on the branch right across from our heads. The pigeons' eyes are small and beady. They are coming right toward us. We need to get our necks out of here, pronto.

Down below, I move my hand around and feel it brush the mushroom cap.

"Guys, I think I can reach the left side of the mushroom," I say. "The one that is supposed to make us smaller."

"But your hand is way down there!" Penny says, looking below us where the rest of our bodies are. We can barely see them through the trees.

"I know what you should do," Robin says quickly. "Grab the left side of the mushroom and rip it into three pieces and toss the pieces up. We'll catch it in our mouths like Steven does at lunch with pinto beans."

"Who's Steven?" Penny asks.

"He's in our class," I say. "Black hair? Green braces?"

Penny looks at me blankly. "I can't be expected to remember everyone I meet."

I roll my eyes. Then I use my hand and manage to rip the piece of mushroom into three. Here goes nothing. I toss all the pieces up.

Our necks are so long and twisty that we can swoop really fast to catch the pieces in our mouths.

Wahoo! We did it! All three of us!

"OW!" I cry as my neck starts shortening so fast that it scrapes against a branch on the way down.

Smaller, smaller, smaller, done.

Finally, my neck is the size it used to be. I turn to Robin and Penny. They're also back to normal. Well, card-sized normal, but at least our necks are even.

Even, Steven.

chapter eight

Tea Time

We say good-bye to the caterpillar and walk toward the pale pink houses, where Penny saw the tea party happening. I hope Frankie is still there by the time we arrive.

"All these houses look alike," I say. "How can we tell which one is the Mad Hatter's?"

"It was three rows back and seven to the side," Penny says. "I counted."

"Oh," I say, surprised and impressed. "That's helpful."

"I wonder why we haven't met Alice yet," Robin says. "Isn't this her story? Where is she?"

I shrug. I'm wondering about that, too.

"Here we are," Penny says when we reach the seventh house in the third row. The house, like all the others, is small and pink and only one level. We can hear sounds of a party coming from the backyard.

"We made it!" I say. "The Mad Hatter's tea party. If Frankie's here, let's be sure to drink the tea right away. I bet that's the magic swallow that will take us home."

"That would be perfect," Penny says. "They'll probably be serving scones and tea sandwiches, too. That's pretty normal for tea parties."

"I love tea sandwiches," Robin says. "Especially little egg salad ones with the crusts cut off."

"Don't forget about the profiteroles," Penny says.

I don't know what those are and I'm not asking. But tea sandwiches sound good. So do scones. I haven't eaten anything normal since we got to Wonderland. Besides the tomato tarts. And those don't count, since they got us into trouble.

Penny, Robin, and I walk around to the back of the house and peer over the fence into the backyard. A big tree is blocking our view, but I can see a table covered with a bright purple polka-dot tablecloth. A short man in a tall hat is sitting on one of the chairs. He's wearing a long jacket, black pants, and a polka-dot bow tie that matches the tablecloth.

"Is that the Mad Hatter?" I ask.

"Yep," Robin says excitedly.

"Guys," I ask hesitantly. "Do you think we need to be careful? If he's angry?"

Penny snort-laughs. "He's not angry. He's *mad*."

"As in bonkers," Robin says.

My cheeks burn. "Oh. Right. I knew that."

"Do you know why he's bonkers?" Penny asks. "It's because in the old days, people who made hats went crazy because of all the fumes and chemicals they ingested."

"Really?" asks Robin. "I didn't know that!"

"Well, I do," says Penny. "I know a lot of stuff. I know you guys think I'm dumb, but I'm not."

"I don't think you're dumb," Robin says.

"Not you," Penny says, lifting her chin. "Abby."

"I don't think you're dumb," I say, my cheeks now on fire. "I'm the one who just sounded dumb, confusing *mad* with *angry*."

Penny shrugs. "Yeah, whatever."

"I . . ." I don't think Penny is dumb. I really don't. I hate that anyone — even Penny — feels like I do. "You just found this house. That was impressive."

"Thanks," Penny says grudgingly.

I look back at the table. Sitting beside the Hatter is a fully dressed rabbit, also in a suit and a bow tie. For a second, I wonder if it *is* the same rabbit who lied to us earlier, but this rabbit is gray instead of white. And on the table, beside the rabbit, is a little brown mouse, who is fast asleep and snoring. Loudly.

"SNORT. SNNOOOOOOORT. SNNOOOOOOOOOORT."

In the middle of the table is a teapot. But I don't see Frankie. Does that mean she's not here?

But then I hear a girl say: "These cookies are delicious."

The girl's voice sounds like Frankie.

Frankie's voice!

IT'S FRANKIE!

Yes, yes, yes! She's really here! We found Frankie!

"Frankie!" I holler from behind the fence. I can't control myself. I'm so happy we found her!

"Abby?" we hear Frankie call. "Is that you?"

"Yes!"

"Where are you?"

"Behind the fence! Behind the part hidden by the tree! I'm with Robin and Penny!"

"My friends are here," we hear Frankie say to the rest of the tea party. "Hurrah!"

In a second, Frankie has dashed over to the fence. She's smiling and looks like her regular Frankie self. Except she's just as tiny as we are.

"It's so good to see you guys!" she cries.

"We've been looking *everywhere* for you," Penny snaps.

"You have?" Frankie says, straightening her glasses on her nose.

"Yes," I say. "And we are so happy we found you! Are you okay? Are you totally freaked out?"

"Hi, Frankie!" Robin chirps. "Isn't this fab? Isn't this balloons?"

Frankie looks at her quizzically. "It *is* fab," she says. "We're in *Alice's Adventures in Wonderland*!"

"We know!" Robin says. "Let me take a picture of all of us back together! Oh. Hmm." She pats her pockets. "My phone is gone. Oh, no! It must have fallen out when we ate the mushrooms!"

"That's too bad," I say. But it isn't really. This way she won't have any proof of where we were when we get back.

"So wait, what happened after you fell down the hole?" I ask Frankie. "Did you panic?"

"Panic? No! Why would I panic?" Frankie smiles. "As soon as I saw the floating furniture, I thought of Alice. By the time I saw the 'Drink Me' sign, I knew I had fallen down the rabbit hole. Do you know how many times I've read *Alice's Adventures in Wonderland* and *Through the Looking Glass*? At least fifteen. Maybe more. This is the most incredible thing that has ever happened to me."

"I know, right?!" Robin cries.

Wow. Frankie is braver than I thought.

"You read the same book fifteen times?" Penny asks, incredulous. "But why?"

I won't admit it, but I kind of see her point. Seems like overkill.

"Are you kidding?" Frankie asks. "Every time I read it, I learn something new. There are so many layers! My dad has read the book even more times than I have! And he says that he understood it in a totally new way when he was in college than when he was a kid, and then again after he had his own kids. He says he gets something different out of it every single time he reads it. And that it even teaches him things about himself."

Really? I don't know about that. A book is a book is a book. But still. Hurrah! We now have someone with us who actually *knows* the story. What a relief. "What's *Through the Looking Glass*?" I ask.

"The sequel," Frankie says. "I love that book, too. I can't believe we're here. Of course I wondered if I was dreaming, but it seemed so real. And then I pinched myself to make sure —"

"We did that, too," Penny says.

"I still think that's bogus," I murmur. "But anyway. Go on."

"And I realized I was awake," Frankie says. "So then I drank the potion and shrank down, and went into the garden to explore. I was looking for Alice, but I don't think she's here yet."

"We must have just missed you," I say.

"How long have we been here, anyway?" Frankie asks.

"At least a few hours," I say.

"My nanny must be freaking out," Penny says. "We have to

figure out what will take us home. My parents will fire her if they find out she lost us, and I can't deal with training someone new. Again."

Frankie nods. "Oh, right. I've been so focused on exploring, I haven't been thinking about how to get out of here."

"Well," I say, "we met the Cheshire Cat and —"

"You did?" Frankie squeals. "I've been looking for him!"

"Yup. And he told us that the right swallow would take us home."

She furrows her brow. "The right swallow? You mean something we have to eat?"

"We think so. Or drink."

She turns back toward the tea party. "It could be the tea."

"But you're still here and you drank some, right?" Penny asks.

"Not yet." Frankie sighs. "I've been trying."

"What's the holdup?" I ask.

"You'll see. It's not exactly a normal tea party."

"Nothing in Wonderland is normal," Penny grumbles.

"This story is kind of bonkers," I say.

"Of course it's bonkers," Frankie says. "That's what makes it so amazing. Just wait until you meet the Hatter, the March Hare, and the Dormouse. They're definitely bonkers."

"All the best people are," we hear the Mad Hatter say.

Frankie pulls opens a gate in the fence I hadn't noticed and says, "You should come in."

Why do I never notice gates in fences? You'd think someone would build them to be more obvious.

We follow her into the backyard.

"Is it okay if my friends join us for tea?" Frankie asks the group.

"I'm afraid we don't have room for them," the Mad Hatter says sadly, shaking his head. His hat veers from side to side. He's shorter than us, but his hat makes him look taller.

Penny narrows her eyes and motions to the many empty seats at the table. "Um. There are like six unused seats."

"Yes, but what if the Dormouse wakes up and wants to sit there?" the Mad Hatter asks, patting the empty seat beside him. "Or there." He gestures to the empty seat next to the empty seat. "Or there or there or there or there! Wait, did I say there?" He points with both hands at the first chair.

"Well, the Dormouse is sleeping," Frankie says, gesturing to the snoring little mouse. "So my friends can sit in those seats and if he wakes up and wants our seats, we'll just move over." She motions for us to sit down before the Hatter can say no.

We all do. No one stops us. Look at Frankie! She's so brave! And in charge! I love it.

"Would you like some chocolate milk?" the gray rabbit — the March Hare — asks me.

Why, yes, I do want some chocolate milk. I'd want chocolate milk even if it's not the right "swallow" to take us home. I look around the table. "Where is it?" I wonder out loud.

"There isn't any," the Mad Hatter says, and bursts out laughing.

"Okay," I say, confused. "Then why did you offer it to me?"

"I didn't offer it," the March Hare says. "I just asked if you would like some."

Frankie gives me an *I told you so* smile.

Penny rolls her eyes.

Robin laughs.

"Got it," I say. "Would it be possible for me to have some tea, please?"

Neither the March Hare nor the Mad Hatter answers.

Maybe I'm just supposed to help myself? I stand up slowly and lean over the table to reach for the teapot.

"It's time to move seats!" the Mad Hatter calls out, looking at his watch.

I drop my hand. Huh?

The Mad Hatter gets up. The March Hare gets up. They both stare at Frankie, Robin, Penny, and me until we all get up. "Everyone move one seat over," the Hatter says.

"Um, why?" I ask.

"Why not?" the Mad Hatter says.

"Exactly," says the March Hare.

Just then, the little brown mouse wakes up.

"Hello!" he squeaks, stretching his little paws above his head. "What did I miss?"

"Everything," the Mad Hatter says at the same time the hare says, "Nothing."

The little mouse yawns. "I think it's time for my nap," he says. He closes his little eyes and goes back to sleep.

The hare picks up a cookie from the plate. "Is this raisin or chocolate chip?"

"Do you have a *raisin* for asking?" asks the Hatter.

The hare nods. "My raisin is that reasons are delicious and chocolate chips are disgusting."

I'm not sure if he mixed those words up on purpose. Also, he's clearly bonkers, because what kind of person in their right mind prefers raisins to chocolate chips?

"They are reasons," the Mad Hatter says. "Reasonably delicious."

"Excellent," the hare says. "Do you think the cookie would eat itself if it knew it was a cookie?"

"Everyone likes cookies, even cookies," the Hatter says.

Robin laughs.

Penny and I glance at each other and shake our heads.

Bonkers, bonkers, bonkers, I mouth.

She smiles. I smile back. Wait. Are Penny and I having a moment?

The Hatter looks at his watch. "It's six o'clock!" he booms. "Time to move places again."

"We just moved places," Frankie says. "Can't we sit for a minute?"

Robin looks startled. "Did you just say it was six o'clock? That's what time my phone said it was, too! But that was ages ago."

"I don't remember," the Mad Hatter says. "But it seems possible. Doesn't it?" he asks the hare.

"It does," says the hare.

"Is it six o'clock or not?" Penny booms.

"Right now?" asks the Hatter.

"Yes! What time is it right now?" I ask. I wish I knew what time it is back home.

He looks back at his watch. "It's . . . um . . . it's . . . it's six o'clock."

"Really?" Frankie asks. She bites her thumbnail again. "But we're all getting picked up at five thirty. Our parents are going to be worried."

"It's okay," I tell them in my most soothing voice. "Time is probably different here. Since we're not in Smithville. That's normal for story hopping."

"Story hopping?" Frankie asks.

Robin nods. "This isn't Abby's first trip into a story.

Normally, she goes into fairy tales. I've been in one, too! I just don't remember."

"Wait, so it might *not* be six back home?" Penny asks.

"Right," I say. "There could be a time difference."

Penny rests her chin in her hand. "So it's like going to Paris. It's six hours ahead there, you know. Although I bet none of you have been to Paris."

"No," I say, feeling the moment between us gone. "None of us have been to Paris."

"But it seems like it's always six o'clock here," Robin says. "That's not a time difference. That's time stopping."

"Where are your watches?" the Mad Hatter asks us.

"I forgot mine at home," I admit.

"Me too," Penny says.

"I don't wear one," Robin and Frankie both say at the same time.

The Mad Hatter's mouth drops open. "You forgot your watch? And *you* don't wear one? But then how do you know the year?"

Huh?

"Um, it's the same year all year," I say slowly.

"Yeah," Robin says. "It's the time that changes."

"I'm sorry to inform you of this, but you are absolutely wrong," the Mad Hatter says. "The time never changes. It's always six o'clock."

I mean . . . seriously?

"Bonkers, bonkers, bonkers," Penny mutters.

"I had a fight with time, you know," the Mad Hatter says. He takes off his hat and scratches his head, then puts his hat back on. "I forget who won."

"I honestly can't tell if he's kidding," I say.

"Oh my goodness," the Hatter says, jumping up. "Did I say it was six o'clock? Let's go, everyone. Move down a seat!"

We all move. Again.

We are never getting the tea. We might be stuck here forever.

"Can I have a sandwich?" Robin asks, staring at the tray of little crustless sandwiches.

"Absolutely not," responds the hare. "Those are for the Dormouse. You can ask him to lend you one when he wakes up."

"Lend her one?" the Mad Hatter asks. "Is she going to give it back?"

"She might," the hare says. "They're pretty old and she might throw it back up."

Penny stands up, her hands shaking. "Okay. That's it. I can't spend one more second in this crazy place. I want to go home — and that means swallowing whatever I have to. Sick-inducing or not."

"Let's do it," I say. "But let's start with the tea. Least likely to make us throw up, I think."

I jump up from my seat and grab the teapot.

"Excuse me," says the hare. "That's very rude."

I don't care. I pour myself a cup. I try not to notice that the teacup is dirty.

I drink it in one gulp. It's cold. And tastes like apple juice. Who knows if this is even tea?

I figure if I suddenly disappear like magic, my friends will know the tea was the correct swallow and they'll drink some and we'll all be home.

Nothing happens.

ARGH.

"Very rude!" the Mad Hatter says. "She didn't even offer us any."

"You put the U in rude," the hare says.

I turn to Frankie, Robin, and Penny. "Well, that didn't work."

"I guess we get to stay a little longer," Robin says with a smile.

"Oh, well," Frankie says, smiling back at Robin.

"What about the tea sandwiches and cookies?" I ask the Mad Hatter. "Can we please try one of each?"

"You can," he says. "But may you?"

"May I?" I ask.

"You may," says the Dormouse, opening his eyes for a split second before going back to sleep.

"You may," repeats the Mad Hatter. "But you may not want to."

ARGH.

Robin's eyes light up. She grabs an egg salad sandwich and pops it in her mouth. She chews. Nothing happens. Absolutely nothing.

Frankie tries a tuna salad sandwich. She doesn't disappear.

Penny hesitates before going for the cream cheese and jelly

one. Nothing happens to her, either. Except she makes a *This is gross* face.

Well, at least I don't have to eat the gross old sandwiches.

I try the cookie.

Yuck. It is reason. I mean raisin. And it doesn't send me home, either.

The Dormouse wakes, yawns, and falls back asleep.

I tried the tea and the cookie. Frankie, Robin, and Penny tried the sandwiches. Nothing worked. So what could be the swallow that will take us home?

"Do you hear that?" asks the hare, putting his hand up to his long ear.

"I think that's me chewing," says Robin, taking another sandwich.

I stop and listen. Actually, I hear something, too. Rustling. And then a voice says:

"The thieves went this way!"

"The thieves?" Penny whispers, her face draining of color. "They're not talking about us, are they?"

"Why would they be talking about you?" Frankie asks.

"We may have eaten the queen's tarts," I say.

Frankie's eyes widen. "You ate the queen's tarts? But . . . but . . . don't you know the poem? None of you read the book?"

"Penny *said* she read the book," I snap.

"You said you read the book, too!" Penny snaps back.

"Just tell us the poem," I say.

Frankie nods and begins reciting:

"*The Queen of Hearts,*
She made some tarts,
All on a summer day:
The Knave of Hearts, he stole those tarts,
And took them quite away!"

"So someone else stole the tarts?" Robin asks, confused.

"Someone else was *supposed* to steal the tarts," Frankie says. "The Knave of Hearts. Which is the Jack. And then he gets caught and the queen puts him on trial. And condemns him to beheading."

Yikes.

"Again with the beheading," Penny says, running her hands over her hair. "Why is this place so obsessed with beheading?"

"That's a very good question." I stand up, feeling sick. "We've got to get out of here before the cards find us."

"Thanks for letting us come to your tea party," Robin tells the Hatter, rubbing her stomach. "The egg salad sandwich was really good."

"It was a pleasure to meet you," Frankie says, jumping out of her seat.

He frowns up at her, then glances from Penny to Robin to me. "Where did you four come from?"

"We've been here the whole time," I say.

He jumps and looks at his watch. "The time? Why, it's six o'clock! Time to move seats for tea!"

"Keep searching!" we hear one of the cards shout in the distance. Eek.

"We've got to move," I say as Frankie, Robin, and I hurry to the gate.

"But where are we running to?" Penny asks, hurrying with us.

"I don't know!" I cry. "Frankie, what happens next in the book?"

Frankie bites her thumbnail as she runs. "Well, now I'm not so sure. The fact that you guys ate the tarts kind of messed up the story."

We messed up the story, huh? I sigh.

Story of my life.

chapter nine

Pig in a Blanket

*t*he four of us dash out of the Mad Hatter's gate and rush along a path in the forest. There are lots of leaves. On the trees, on the ground. The leaves are all different colors. But not like in the fall. These leaves are neon pink, neon yellow, and some are even striped, or covered in polka dots. It's kind of cool, but it's not helping my state of mind much.

"Yup," Frankie says. "The knave was supposed to steal the tarts. Not you guys."

"Great," I say. "Just great."

"Why did the knave steal the queen's tarts anyway?" Robin asks.

"I don't know," Frankie says. "Because he was hungry? They never say. In the real story, when the knave is on trial, Alice has to testify in court. But then she gets attacked by all the cards, and all of a sudden, she wakes up — she's back outside with her sister. It was just a dream."

My mouth drops open. "A dream? This whole thing is a dream?"

Frankie nods.

"So we're stuck inside someone's dream," I say. I guess that explains the striped and polka-dot leaves, and the clouds that dance, and the weird flying food. "But if we stole the tarts before the knave got to them, then we must have fallen into the story *before* Alice. How does Wonderland exist if she hasn't dreamt it yet?" I ask, frowning.

"Maybe Wonderland is real," Robin says, her eyes sparkling. "Alice may be dreaming, but that doesn't mean the place doesn't exist."

I'm getting a headache.

"Girls, we have to focus," Penny says, looking around. "What else is there to swallow in the story?"

"There are a ton of things to swallow," Frankie says. "There are mushrooms —"

"Tried those," Robin says. "Hey, what about a leaf?"

"The colorful ones on the trees?" I ask.

"Yeah! I'm sure they taste just like lettuce," Robin says.

I raise an eyebrow. "Um, you first," I say. I do not want to eat a leaf. Especially a weirdly patterned leaf.

Robin and Frankie run up ahead to a tree with neon pink leaves. I watch as they each rip a leaf off a branch and take a bite.

I really am so impressed with Frankie. I definitely underestimated her. She might be shy, but underneath she's also fearless.

I watch their faces for a reaction. Robin wrinkles her nose. Frankie coughs and spits out her leaf.

Neither of them disappears.

"Didn't work, huh?" I ask.

"Probably needed dressing," Penny says.

I can't help but laugh.

"You haven't been to the Duchess's house yet, have you?" Frankie asks, wiping her lips with the back of her hand. "Or the rabbit's?"

"No," I say. "But I don't exactly trust the rabbit."

"We should look for their houses," Frankie says. "They both have things we can swallow."

Robin and Frankie trot up ahead, arm in arm, so I wind up walking beside Penny.

She sighs. Loudly.

"Don't worry," I say. "We'll get home. I always do. At least, I always have."

She sighs again. "But everything is different this time, isn't it?"

"Yeah," I say. "I guess it is."

"I just hate being stuck."

"Have you ever been stuck somewhere before?" I ask.

"Yes." She hesitates. "Do you want to know a secret?"

"I guess," I say. Is Penny about to tell me that *she* goes into stories sometimes, too?

Her cheeks turn red. "My first week of kindergarten, I got stuck in the girls' bathroom. The stall door got jammed. And no one was there to help me."

Oh. That sounds awful.

"You couldn't slide under the door?" I ask.

"It was the one on the second floor. You know the stall all the way to the right? The door goes down to the bottom. I was totally stuck."

"Yikes. So what happened?"

"It was a field trip day. And all the other kids went to get on the bus. The teacher didn't know us all then, since it was the first week of school. He counted the kids wrong and no one knew I was missing. So the bus left."

I gasp. "And you were still in the bathroom?"

She nods.

"For how long?"

"At least an hour. Maybe more. Finally, a first-grade teacher came in and heard me banging, and she had to call the janitor and he helped me out. But it took forever."

"Did the teacher realize you were missing?"

"Yes," she says. "Eventually."

"Did you get to go on the field trip?"

She shakes her head. "I was so freaked out, they called my parents to pick me up. But they were traveling. Obviously. They're always traveling. My old nanny finally came and got me like a half hour later."

"That's a terrible memory," I say, stepping on a pile of leaves.

She giggles. "It's kind of funny, though. I've never told anyone that story," she adds.

"No one ever found out?"

"No! I didn't want to be known as Bathroom Girl in the first week of school. Nicknames stick, you know."

"I guess," I say. "I promise not to call you Bathroom Girl."

"Thanks," Penny says.

"But we can call Robin and Frankie Leaf Eaters if you want."

She laughs, and I laugh, too.

"Being stuck in Wonderland isn't as bad as being stuck in the bathroom, though, right?" I point out. I notice Frankie and Robin coming to a stop down the path, in front of a small brick house.

"True," Penny says. "It's just . . . it's so *weird* here! There are no rules. And I like rules. I know that sounds strange since my parents don't have any. But I like plans. I like things that make sense. And this place makes no sense." Her shoulders droop. "You probably think *I'm* weird."

I shake my head. "I don't think you're weird at all. I'm the same. I love rules. I am all about rules."

Wait. Do Penny and I have something in common?

I think about what Frankie said about books having layers.

I guess people have layers, too. And only when you dig deeper, when you really get to know the person, do you discover what those layers are.

Hmmm.

Up ahead, Frankie turns around and motions for us to join her and Robin at the door to the house.

"I think this is the Duchess's house," Frankie whispers, pointing to a baby carriage parked by the entrance. "We're going to try and swallow her soup."

"Wait, does the Duchess have a baby?" I ask. "Is that how you know this is her house?"

"Yes!" Frankie says. Then she cocks her head to the side. "Well . . . she kind of has a baby."

"Huh?"

Frankie smiles to herself. "You'll see."

Robin steps up to the front door and knocks twice.

A woman wearing a poofy red velvet dress answers. She has a very large head and short curly blond hair and a long, pointy nose. She's holding a baby wrapped in a yellow blanket.

Except . . . I stare at the baby. It's not a baby.

It's a pig. An actual pig. A baby pig? A pig in a blanket?

Ha, ha, ha.

It's a real-life pig in a blanket! And not a teeny, tiny hot dog that my brother would insist should be called a dog in a blanket.

He's not wrong. It does make more sense.

I miss Jonah.

"Who are you?" the woman snaps, glaring at all four of us.

"I'm, um, Abby," I say. "And these are my friends Penny, Frankie, and Robin." Wait. Did I just refer to Penny as my friend?

"And you're the Duchess," Frankie says to the woman. "Hi!"

"Of course I'm the Duchess!" the woman mutters. "Who else would I be? Are you coming in or not? You shall tell me why you're here while I rock the baby to sleep."

I try to peek into the blanket to get a look at the pig, who's wide wake. He's pink with a little brown nose. He is pretty cute.

We walk into a kitchen. A man in a backward apron is cooking something in a big pot on the stove. And another guy is sitting at the table. He's short and skinny, with a mustache and long hair. He's wearing flared jeans, a fringy vest, and purple sunglasses. He reminds me of old pictures I've seen of my grandpa and great-uncle. Back from the . . . 1970s?

This guy looks around college age. I wonder if there's college in Wonderland.

"Hi," Robin says to the guy. She introduces herself and all of us.

"Hey. I'm Cliff." The guy lets out a sigh.

"Who's Cliff?" I whisper to Frankie.

"I don't remember a Cliff in the book at all," Frankie says, biting her fingernail. "I'm kind of confused."

"I don't remember a Cliff from the parts I skimmed, either," Penny whispers.

"And there's no Cliff in the movie," Robin adds, also in a whisper.

Weird. So where did Cliff come from? And where is Alice?

The Duchess sits down in a rocking chair near the window and rocks the baby. I mean, er, the pig-baby.

Penny steps closer to stand by the Duchess. "Who's a cute piglet?" Penny says. "Who, who? Aww, look at its tiny piglet ears. Its cute little nose is twitching!" Her face is radiating joy. "I've always wanted a pig," she says. "When I grow up, I'm going to have a farm with pigs. And goats."

"And don't forget horses," Frankie says.

"Obviously horses," Penny says, and goes back to cooing at the pig-baby.

Penny is acting like it's totally normal for a lady in a fancy dress to be rocking a piglet. I thought she liked things that made sense?

"Oink, oink," the pig-baby says.

"You are such a piggy!" the Duchess says a little meanly to the piglet. The piglet oinks again.

"Can I hold him?" Penny asks the Duchess.

"Please." The Duchess passes the pig to Penny.

"You are so sweet," Penny coos to the piglet. "Do you guys want to hold him, too?" she asks me, Robin, and Frankie.

"Um, that's okay," I say. The pig kind of smells like poop. "I'm not much of a pig person."

"Where is lunch?" the Duchess calls to the cook. "The baby and I are hungry."

"The soup is almost ready, Duchess," the cook says, stirring the large blue pot on the stove.

Yes! The soup Frankie mentioned is about to be served. Which means maybe, hopefully, we will soon be on our way home! Yes, yes, yes!

Penny oohs and ahhs over the piglet and keeps talking about its "adorable, velvety pink ears." Frankie and Robin finally go over to look at the pig-baby, too.

I walk to the stove to check out the soup. It's bubbling away, and is a pretty golden color. Whew. Maybe we can finally eat something normal.

"Do you know what this soup needs?" the cook asks.

"What?" I ask.

"Pepper." He takes out a mill and starts to add pepper to the soup. And more pepper. And even more pepper. The soup is turning black with pepper. Pepper is somehow flying around the room.

"Achoo!" sneeze Robin, Frankie, and Penny.

"Oink-choo!" sneezes the pig-baby.

"Achoo!" sneezes the Duchess. "That's enough pepper."

But the cook doesn't stop grinding.

"I said that's enough pepper," the Duchess repeats, her voice rising.

The pepper tickles my nose. "Achoo!" I sneeze. It really is enough pepper.

"Everyone likes pepper," the cook says, continuing to grind. At this point, the pot looks like it has more pepper in it than soup. "Yum-yum," he says.

The Duchess jumps over to the cook and pulls on his arm. "Enough!"

The sudden motion makes the cook yank his arm back, and suddenly the entire pot of soup tips over. Black-brown pepper soup floods the floor. The pot is resting upside down in the middle of the mess.

"Nooo!" I yell. "That was our way home!"

The Duchess slips on the soup, flies backward, and lands on her behind. "Ouch!"

This is not good. Not good at all.

"But we have to eat the soup!" I call out.

Frankie and Robin and I look at one another, concern in our eyes. Penny is too busy cooing at the pig-baby.

"What do we do?" Frankie asks.

The three of us look down at the soup-coated floor.

Then we all grimace.

"No," I say. Is that our only option? Are we going to have to — ugh — lick the floor?

Frankie makes a face.

No. Way. We can't do it. We cannot lick the floor. I would rather stay in Wonderland than lick the floor.

If only Prince were here. He'd lick the floor.

Hey, so would Jonah.

Suddenly, Frankie's eyes light up. "The pot! We can lick the pot!"

"Of course," I say. "The pot! I'll lick the pot!" I love licking pots. At home, I'm always asking to lick the pot. Usually, there's mac and cheese in it, but beggars can't be choosers. I pick the pot up off the floor. "Ouch!"

It's hot.

Wait a sec. I don't lick the pot at home. I lick the bowl. Or the spoon. Plus, if I lick the pot now, I will burn my tongue off. "We have to wait until it cools down," I say.

"Oink-choo!" sneezes the pig.

"Bless you," says Penny.

"Is someone going to clean that up?" the Duchess asks.

"It was your fault," huffs the cook.

Frankie sits down at the table right across from Cliff. He's been quiet this whole time.

"So who are you, again?" she asks him. "I'm so sorry, but I don't remember you from *Alice's Adventures in Wonderland*."

"I wasn't in the original book," Cliff says. And then he sneezes.

"Gesundheit," says the Duchess.

"Bless you," Frankie says, and Cliff nods. "I know," she tells him. "Then why *are* you here? How are you here?"

All of a sudden, I hear a noise outside. I glance out the window and see a bunch of card-people in the distance. The Eight, Nine, and Ten of Clubs are approaching the house. Ack!

"Uh, guys, we're going to have to go really soon," I say. I quickly stick my index finger inside the pot — luckily it's not too hot anymore — and then I lick my finger.

That's a lot of pepper.

I swallow and I wait, closing my eyes. Then I sneeze.

"Gesundheit," the Duchess says.

"Since I heard that, I guess I am still here," I say.

"You are," says Frankie.

There's banging on the front door.

Crumbs.

"We have to leave," I tell Penny. "Come on, give the Duchess back the pig-baby. The cards are here!"

"But he likes me," Penny says and makes a sad face.

"Who is it?" asks the Duchess, heading for the door.

"We're looking for the thieves!" screams Ten. "The tart thieves!"

"Are there any tart thieves here?" the Duchess asks, turning around to face the rest of us.

"No," Frankie, Robin, and I all say at the same time. Penny keeps cooing at the pig-baby.

"Penny," I whisper. "We have to go. Now."

Penny makes another sad face and passes the pig-baby back to the Duchess.

"Oink!" screams the pig.

"I wish I could go, too," Cliff says sadly. "I was trapped! And now I'm stuck here forever!"

I freeze at the word *trapped*. "Who trapped you?" I ask him.

"An evil fairy," he says.

An evil fairy? What? Could Cliff be trapped here the same way Maryose is trapped in the magic mirror in my basement?

But what raisin — reason — did an evil fairy have for trapping him here?

I glance out the window. The cards look like they're about to push through the front door.

"Cliff!" I say. "We're trying to escape, too. Come with us!"

"There's no way out," he says.

"There is!" I exclaim. "We just have to swallow the right thing. The Cheshire Cat told us so."

"I've tried that," he says. "I've swallowed everything. The Cheshire Cat gave me the same riddle he gave you. And I've been stuck here for over forty years."

My heart sinks. "Are you serious?"

"Yeah, man," he says. "As serious as Watergate."

Huh?

There's no time to figure out what he's talking about. We've got to run.

chapter ten

And the Cat Came Back

Penny, Robin, Frankie, and I sprint through the forest until we're wheezing and out of breath. I don't hear footsteps behind us. I think we lost the cards. That was close. This is getting scary. We *have* to find our way out before they catch us.

I like my head just where it is. On my neck.

"We need to get to the rabbit's house," Frankie says, panting a little. "That may be our last chance to swallow the right thing."

"Let's rest for a minute first," Robin suggests, holding her side.

We find a shady spot to hide. The four of us sit on a bed of fuchsia and electric blue leaves in a shallow ditch, hidden from the path by bushes.

I can't stop thinking about Cliff. Who trapped him, exactly? Was he really cursed? Did the same fairy who cursed and trapped Maryrose curse and trap Cliff? Could we get cursed and trapped, too? Is there really no way out?

Why are we here anyway? What if it wasn't Maryrose who brought us to Wonderland?

"Oh, yay!" Robin says.

"What are you yaying about?" I ask. I am not feeling anything to yay about.

"He's back!" Robin cheers. She's motioning directly across from us.

I look over. The Cheshire Cat is there, resting on his side, on a thin brown branch.

Frankie jumps up. "It's the Cheshire Cat! Most of him, anyway. I don't see his tail."

"Then you're not looking hard enough," the cat responds. His tail — which *really* wasn't there a second ago — swishes out from underneath him.

Penny crosses her arms over her chest. She's about as excited by the riddle-speaking cat as I am. Not very.

"Mr. Cat," I say. "Do you know Cliff?"

"Sure do," the cat responds.

"He said he's been trying to find the right swallow for decades and hasn't been able to."

"There's cliff now," the cat says and lifts his furry chin.

What? I whirl around. I don't see Cliff. I only see . . . an actual cliff behind us. The cat laughs.

Penny groans.

"I didn't mean a cliff-cliff," I say. "I mean the guy named Cliff. Do you know him or not? He's wearing bell-bottom jeans? He has brown hair?"

"The hare is with the Hatter," says the cat.

"No!" I say. "*Hair*. Brown hair? Like mine," I add, grabbing a fistful of my curly tendrils.

The Cheshire Cat shakes his head. "If you think your hair is a rabbit, I can't help you, child."

I give up. Seriously, I give up.

"Mr. Cheshire Cat," Frankie says. "Forget the hare —"

The cat eyes Frankie. "How can I forget the hair? It's on your head. Did you forget your hair somewhere? Do you need help finding it?"

Penny slaps a hand against her forehead.

"Listen, Mr. Cat," I say. "You told us a swallow would take us back home. So far, we've swallowed tarts, tea, sandwiches, leaves, potions, mushrooms, a cookie, and soup. But we're still here."

"Are you?" the cat says. He begins disappearing slowly, his body fading first and then his grin lingering before it vanishes, too.

Penny stomps her foot against the leaves. "Abby, you chased him away!"

"I did not! I needed to get some answers!"

Robin sits down on a log. "Abby, why can't you and Penny just calm down? This is fun. Let's hang out!"

"Hang out *here*?" I say, staring at her. "Robin, the cards are after us! The queen is going to chop off our heads!"

"All the movies have a happy ending," she says, twirling her ponytail. "I'm sure we will, too."

"This isn't a movie, Robin!" Penny cries. "This is real life!"

Yeah. Exactly. I never expected to be on Penny's side about anything. But she's right! *I'm* right!

"Calm down, you guys," Robin says. "We can't take this out on each other."

"This is all Frankie's fault," Penny grumbles.

Frankie gasps.

"Hey!" I yell, facing Penny. "She didn't mean to fall into the hole."

"Then she should have looked where she was going!" Penny snaps, taking a step toward me.

"*You* shouldn't have made us play cards outside when it was so windy!" I retort, jabbing my finger at her. "I told you it was windy. But did you listen? Noooo."

Frankie and Robin back away, pretending to have great interest in a berry tree.

"You're such a know-it-all!" Penny cries.

"I'm such a know-it-all? *You're* such a know-it-all. And you're so bossy!"

"You're the bossiest person who ever lived!" Penny says, her cheeks bright red. "And you scared the Cheshire Cat away before he could tell us how to get home!"

Suddenly, the cat reappears on the tree branch. With his big grin.

"You're back," Frankie says, clapping her hands together. "Mr. Cheshire Cat, can you tell us where to find the rabbit's house?"

"It's one thousand feet ahead and three hundred feet that aren't right," he says.

Huh?

"What does that *mean*?" Penny demands. "What's not right?"

The cat disappears again. This time, his grin is the first to go.

"Crumbs," Penny mutters, kicking a pebble.

Seriously? "Stop stealing my word!"

"You can't steal a word, Abby," she says. "But fine. I won't say 'crumbs' if it means that much to you. I won't use your precious word."

"Good. Don't!" If we don't get out of here soon, I'm going to end up beheading Penny.

The cat appears again. I get excited, but he disappears just as quickly. Then appears. Then disappears.

Ah! "Stop doing that!" I yell.

"*Hare* today, gone tomorrow," says the Cheshire Cat, appearing once more. "Am I or am I not?"

"Look, Mr. Cat," Frankie says. "I'm sorry my friends are arguing. Is there *anything* else you can tell us about how to get home?"

"The surprise was a disguise you saw with your eyes," the cat responds.

My head hurts. I can't tell if he's giving us more clues or just being annoying.

The surprise was a disguise you saw with your eyes? What does that even mean?

Before I can ask, the cat — of course — disappears.

This time, he doesn't come back.

chapter eleven

Let Them Eat Cake

One thousand feet ahead," Frankie repeats. "How do we figure out how far that is? I'm about four feet."

"Oh! I bet he means actual feet," Robin says, pointing downward. "Everything he says is always the other meaning of the word."

So we walk forward, one foot in front of the other, counting to ourselves. "Nine hundred and ninety-eight. Nine hundred and ninety-nine. One thousand!" I call out. "What's next?"

"Three hundred feet that aren't right," Penny says. "Do we walk back three hundred feet? That sounds like a waste of time."

"Do you know what's not right?" Robin exclaims. "Left!"

"Right!" Frankie says. "I mean, smart!"

"Robin, you are really good at riddles," I say, impressed. I didn't know that, and I thought I knew everything about her.

She blushes happily. I guess Robin has layers, too.

We turn to the left. Luckily, there's a path. We take three hundred more steps and then, out of nowhere, we see another house. It must be the rabbit's house!

"Robin solved the riddle!" Frankie says. "Way to go."

"Wahoo!" we all cheer.

As we get closer, we see that the house is more a hut than a house. It's oval and made of stone, packed dirt, twigs, and leaves. There's a small chimney and several windows without any glass panes. If we weren't tiny, we would not be able to fit inside the house at all.

"Mr. Rabbit? Are you home?" Frankie asks. She knocks once, and then pushes open the door just enough for all of us to look inside.

I don't see anyone. Or hear anyone. But the house looks cozy. There's a yellow sofa with throw pillows and a colorful rug. Two rocking chairs. And a toy area in one corner with building blocks. We all squeeze through the door and walk inside.

I look at the walls, which are covered in framed photographs of the White Rabbit and his family. I look more closely. The rabbit is wearing a coat and eyeglasses.

"I know we came here on purpose," I say. "But I'm not sure we should trust the rabbit. He *is* the one who told us to eat the tarts."

"His house feels friendly, though," Robin points out.

It's true. I stop in front of the picture of two white rabbits, one in a tuxedo and the other in a long white dress and veil, about to cut a big carrot. I guess a carrot is like a wedding cake for rabbits. Other pictures show their seven children, all very cute with floppy ears. A sign above the kitchen doorway says: A CARROT A DAY KEEPS THE DOCTOR AWAY.

Another wall has photographs of famous rabbits. I see Peter Rabbit. Bugs Bunny. Rabbit from *Winnie-the-Pooh*. And the Easter bunny, holding a basket full of colorful eggs. On a bookshelf are many books, all with rabbit-related titles. *How to Talk to Anybunny. Be the Best Hopper. Raising Li'l Rabbits Right.*

"Ooh, check out what's on that table!" Penny says.

The rest of us walk over to see. There's a small bottle on the table. With a label that says: DRINK ME.

And next to the bottle are four little glasses! Meant for us? Probably, right?

Could this finally be the swallow to take us home? Or is it some crazy potion?

"This better not make us smaller," I say.

Frankie shakes her head. "Since the last potion we drank made us small, maybe this one will make us normal size again."

Penny opens the bottle. She sniffs it. "Yuck. Carrot smoothie. I hate carrots."

I take the bottle and smell it. She's right. The potion is green, not orange, but it does smell like carrots. I have a brief flashback to the time I fell into *Hansel and Gretel* and was force-fed veggie smoothies. Blah.

I pour a little of the potion into each glass.

"Cheers," I say, and we all clink glasses. Then we each take a sip. The potion definitely tastes like carrots. Penny must not be pleased.

Suddenly, my shoulders are growing as wide as the room. My neck is going back up, up, up, but this time, the rest of me is getting huge, too! My feet look like my dad's. Wait — they look like five times the size of my dad's.

"AHHH!" we all cry.

We're GIANTS.

I'm so big that I have to hunch over along the ceiling. My arm is so long it goes right out the window, which, thankfully, has no glass.

Frankie, Robin, and Penny are giants, too. One of Frankie's arms snakes right up the chimney. Robin's leg is through the side door. Penny's hand goes out another window.

We're wedged inside the house. I can barely move.

THIS IS NOT GOOD.

"What is that infernal racket!" an annoyed voice calls from down the hall.

The White Rabbit comes storming out of the bedroom. He's wearing his little round eyeglasses. His wife, in a pink-striped bathrobe, and seven little rabbits in pajamas are behind him.

My elbow keeps growing. I'm about to knock over all the rabbits.

"AHH!" the rabbits shout and rush out the front door in the nick of time.

"Sorry!" I call to them.

"Hey! This is our house!" the White Rabbit shouts from the front lawn. "Get out!"

If we could, we would.

"Take that!" the White Rabbit says, and throws a rock at my arm.

"Ow!" I cry. "Stop that!"

The White Rabbit is scowling at me. "No! You stop growing in my house this instant. Get out!"

Mama Rabbit throws a rock at Robin's foot. Then all the rabbit kids pick up pebbles and rocks and start flinging them at us.

"Is she really teaching her kids to throw rocks?" I ask. "Great parenting! You're raising bullies! Is this how you raise little rabbits right?"

"Ow!" Penny says. "I can't even move my leg to rub where the rock hit my shin!"

"Stop it!" Frankie yells as a pebble hits her in the arm.

Wait. What was that? Something soft just landed right on my foot that's sticking out the window. Something that smells good. I sniff the air. Is that cake?

Another glob of something lands on my arm. It's definitely cake.

Why are the White Rabbit and his family throwing rocks and cake at us? This makes no sense! Even for Wonderland!

I'm able to turn my face just enough to see the White Rabbit standing right outside, ready to throw another little cake at me. Where is he getting the cakes from, anyway?

"Scram!" the rabbit says, throwing more cake. It lands right on my hand.

I am so bent over just under the ceiling that I'm afraid my head will go through the roof!

"Listen, Mr. Rabbit," I say. "Why did you tell us to eat the queen's tarts? Were you trying to get us into trouble?" I ask.

"I did no such thing!" the rabbit says.

"Liar, liar, bunny pants on fire!" Penny shouts. "We all heard you!"

The rabbit frowns. "I've never seen you or these other giants before in my life!"

"You did so see us!" Penny says, all hunched over. Her elbow goes through another window. "We were smaller then. In the garden?"

"Huh?" the rabbit says. "I have no idea what you're talking about! I've never seen you four before — at any size. Now get out of my house!"

He IS the White Rabbit from the queen's garden. I saw him with my own eyes! Same face. Same pink nose. Same floppy ears and little round eyeglasses. He's right in front of me now.

But I can tell by his expression that he doesn't know who we are. His brow is furrowed and he's frowning. He reaches into the pocket of his robe and pulls out a tiny carrot and begins munching on it distractedly.

"Wait a sec," Penny says. "I thought you hated carrots! The rabbit we met earlier said he hated carrots! Remember?!"

I gasp. She's right. And . . . what was it the Cheshire Cat said? *The surprise was a disguise you saw with your eyes.*

Could the Cheshire Cat have meant the White Rabbit? Maybe the rabbit who told us to eat the tarts was in disguise — as THIS white rabbit. Maybe *that* rabbit was someone else entirely?

But who? And why? Who would want to get us in trouble with the queen?

"Oh, goodness! Oh, dear!" the rabbit says. He looks at his pocket watch. "I'm very late. I must go! Bye!"

148

The rabbit rushes off. But his wife and seven bunny children are still glaring at us. The kids keep throwing cake at us. A piece lands on my chin. I stick out my tongue — might as well taste it and see if it's the right swallow — but my tongue can't reach.

Penny's face is now so big it's blocking the doorway. I can barely see out the window.

"Take that, freaky giant girls!" a bunny kid says and flings a piece of cake at Penny. It goes right into her mouth.

"Argh!" Penny barely manages to say.

"Penny!" I cry. "Are you all right?" Doesn't that bunny kid know throwing food into people's mouths is a choking hazard?

She's swallowing. Which is a super-loud sound when a giant does it.

"Not bad," she says, licking her lips. "Chocolate peanut-butter!"

"It's a good thing you're not allergic to peanuts," I say. Haven't they heard of nut-free in Wonderland?

"Oh!" she calls out as her hand suddenly comes out of the window. Her foot comes down from the chimney. "I'm shrinking!"

Could Penny be shrinking because she swallowed the cake?

A bunny kid pulls his arm back and pitches a piece of cake right at my face. It lands on my cheek. Ew, sticky! But it really smells delicious. I manage to swipe it off with my tongue and take a nibble. "Yum, that *is* good."

And it works! *My* arms start shrinking. My foot comes out of the window. I'm suddenly standing straight up.

Two bunny girls throw pieces of cake at Frankie and Robin. They quickly take licks.

We're all card-sized again. I arch my back and rub it. Being a giant is achy.

"I'm calling the guard-cards!" Mama Rabbit says. "They'll arrest the intruders!"

One of the rabbit kids is glaring at us. "Yeah! You're toast!"

"You have toast?" Penny asks. "Can we swallow some?"

"No! Run!" I yell. We scurry out the front door. The bunny kids are chasing us.

Right outside the door is a mouse. A huge mouse. Well, probably a normal-sized mouse that looks huge because we're tiny.

"Are you the ones who ate the tarts?" the mouse asks.

"Um . . ." Penny hesitates.

"Don't answer!" I hiss. "The mouse might be working for the cards!"

"The cards saw us eat the tarts with their own eyes," Robin points out.

Forget the fact that cards shouldn't even have eyes in the first place. "I don't know what they actually saw," I say. I am trying to think like a lawyer. "Just don't admit anything. They'll use it against us!"

"If you did, I'll help you," the mouse says. "Climb up on my back and I'll get you out of here!"

"Should we believe him?" Robin asks me.

"Grab them!" one of the bunnies says, coming up behind us.

"Believe him!" I say, and jump on the mouse. What other choice do we have? Robin, Frankie, and Penny jump on behind me, and the mouse takes off bounding down the path.

"This is weird," Frankie says.

"This is wild!" Robin adds.

"This is FUN," Penny says, with a giggle.

"Really?" I ask, staring back at her. "Being curved around

the ceiling of a house was fun? Being pelted with rocks was fun? Riding a mouse is fun?"

Penny laughs. "It kind of is," she says, holding on tight. "Don't you think?"

"I kind of do," I admit as we zoom through Wonderland. Maybe this place isn't so bad after all.

chapter twelve

So Many Questions

Soon, the angry bunnies are far behind us. This mouse is *fast*.

"What do you guys think?" I ask my friends as we bounce around on the mouse's back. We all hold on to his fur tight. It doesn't seem to bother him. "Was the White Rabbit who told us to eat the queen's tarts a fake?" I explain my theory about the first rabbit we met being in disguise.

"But why would he disguise himself as the White Rabbit?" Robin asks.

"He clearly wanted us to eat the tarts," Penny says. "Maybe he wanted us to get in trouble."

"But why?" Frankie asks as we zoom under a branch.

"Maybe he's trying to trap us," I say, shivering. *Trapped.* Like poor Cliff.

The mouse comes to a stop at a quiet clearing. The ground is covered with grass, so it makes for a soft landing when we all jump off the mouse's back.

"Thanks for the lift," I say.

"Anytime," the mouse says. "My friends and I are all impressed that you took a stand against the queen. You girls are brave. We'll help you any way we can."

"We're trying to find something magical to eat," Frankie says. "Any suggestions?"

"Is there a Wonderland restaurant?" I ask. "McWonderland?"

The mouse shrugs its mouse shoulders. "I only eat stuff I find on the ground. Ooh, there's a seed!"

I am not eating a seed off the ground. That's where I draw the line. Even Jonah wouldn't eat that. Unless it was covered in ketchup.

The mouse nibbles on the seed thoughtfully. "Maybe my

friends can help," he says, looking around. "Guys?" he calls out. "Any ideas?"

Suddenly, a bunch of little animals emerge from behind the trees — a duck, a rat, birds. They're all chattering. And they're all our size, too. It's like a magical zoo.

The duck waddles over to us. "Nope, I have no ideas," he says. "But I bet the tart was good, huh? I've always wanted to try a queen's tart."

"It was only so-so," Robin tells him. "It was a tomato tart. Why would someone make a tomato tart, anyway?"

A rainbow-colored baby parrot flaps over to us from the tree branch above.

"Can I rest on your shoulder?" the parrot asks Penny. "I'm very light."

"Sure," Penny says, beaming. "I love your feathers."

"Me too," he preens.

Another rainbow-colored baby parrot lands on me. I can feel his claws on my shoulder and his soft feathers on my cheek. He isn't *that* light. Um, maybe his parents could come get him now?

"These birds are amazing," Penny says. "My grandmother

had tons of birds as pets. Ooh, there's a pink hummingbird," she adds, pointing up to the branches. "And a yellow canary! And look at that one!" she says, pointing to a blue-and-white bird perched on a branch. "Does anyone know what kind of bird that is?"

"Hmm," Frankie says. "I've read about that kind of bird before. I forget what it's called. Let me think . . ."

"Who cares about that one?" the baby parrot on Penny's shoulder says, frowning. "He's only *two* colors. I'm a whole rainbow."

The parrot on my shoulder finally flies off. Ahh. Better.

"Does your grandma live in Smithville?" I ask Penny. "You talk about her a lot."

She shakes her head. "No. I mean, she used to. But . . ." She hangs her head. "She died a few years ago."

"Oh, no," I say softy. "I'm sorry."

"Yeah. Me too." She sighs. "My mom was really close with her, too. And ever since my grandma died . . . well, my mom doesn't want to be around that much."

Poor Penny. I miss my nana, too, since she lives across the country, but at least I can speak to her whenever I want.

A grown-up rainbow parrot flies over and tells the other birds that the Four of Diamonds is feeding bread to the ducks at the pond. All the birds start to fly away. The mouse and the duck get ready to go, too.

"We won't rat you out!" the blue-and-white bird says as he soars away. "Promise!"

"I won't, either," says a small gray creature by my foot. "And I *am* a rat."

"Good luck," says the big mouse before he bounds away. "See you later, alligator!"

I close my eyes. "Please tell me there's not an alligator behind me."

"I think this time it really was just a figure of speech," Penny says, laughing.

"So what now?" Robin asks when all the animals have gone. We start walking again.

"Frankie, is there *anything* left in the story that we could eat?" I ask.

Frankie bites her thumbnail. "I don't know. We've kind of been going through the book backward. We started at the queen's garden and then we went to the tea party, and then we went to the Duchess's house and the White Rabbit's house . . . and I think we just met all the animals that Alice met when she flooded the forest with her tears . . . which means . . . Look! A door!"

Straight ahead, surrounded by trees, is, in fact, a door. A shiny blue door. Attached to nothing, though. Just a door. How could a door just be there?

"Should we go inside?" I wonder.

"Don't you see?" Frankie says. "It's one of the blue doors from the beginning! We've come full circle!"

She throws open the door and runs inside.

Robin pushes her way in next, and Penny and I follow.

Yup. It's the long hallway with the banana-yellow ceiling, the chessboard walls, and all the blue doors. This is where we landed when we first fell into Wonderland. We did come full circle. My heart sinks.

We must have gone through everything in Wonderland if we're back here. And nothing we drank or ate was the swallow to bring us home.

I feel panicky. Did the Cheshire Cat lie to us? Was Cliff right?

Were we tricked? Is anyone who they say they are? Are we trapped here forever? Trapped like Maryrose in my mirror?

"Well, hello," says the White Rabbit. He's sitting on the glass table, wearing his red coat and little round eyeglasses. His legs are swinging beneath him and he's looking at his pocket watch. The DRINK ME sign is on the table, next to the bottle of potion.

Huh? Where did he come from? Was he here when we came in? Or did he just appear?

I narrow my eyes at him. "Which rabbit are you?" I ask. "Are you the REAL White Rabbit or the FAKE White Rabbit?"

"The real one of course," he insists. "There's only one rabbit! And it's me!"

"How do we know for sure?" Penny asks, hands on her hips. "Prove it!"

PLOP!

Thud.

What was that sound?

It sounded like something falling onto the ground . . . just like when we fell in.

I turn around. A creature about our height has landed at the far end of the hallway. It comes hopping down toward us.

Oh, wow.

It's another White Rabbit. He's also wearing a red coat and little round eyeglasses. He looks EXACTLY like the rabbit sitting on the table.

This White Rabbit glares at us as he hops closer. "You four again? How'd you make it out of my house?"

"Wait. Are *you* the real rabbit?" Frankie asks him.

"Of course I am!" he says. He studies the other rabbit. "Who are you?"

"Who are *you*?" the other rabbit asks.

My head hurts. The first rabbit said HE was the real rabbit. But the one who just fell into the hallway recognized us from his house.

Which is the real one and which is the pretend one?

I stare at both rabbits. They look exactly the same. How can I know who is telling the truth?

Suddenly, there's another noise:

PLOP!

Thud.

"OOF!"

We all look over to see who could have fallen in this time. It better not be a third rabbit.

No. It's a girl.

She is wearing a blue dress with a white smock. She's a little younger than us. I'm guessing she's around seven. Jonah's age.

"Oh, my," the girl says, brushing back her blond hair. "Where am I? I fell down a rabbit hole!"

Penny gasps.

"OMG!" Frankie cries.

"Oh wow oh wow oh wow!" says Robin.

Oh, wow is right.

The girl is Alice.

chapter thirteen

Hello, Alice

Alice! THE Alice! In Wonderland!

She's finally here!

"It's her!" Robin murmurs, her eyes wide.

"Shhh," I say. "Don't interrupt the story. If she doesn't see us, maybe her story can continue the way it's supposed to."

Alice doesn't seem to see us. That's because we're all still tiny, so we're basically down by her feet. So are the two White Rabbits.

Alice frowns at the table with the DRINK ME sign.

"Oh! I am very thirsty," Alice says, going over to the table.

She picks up the bottle. "It does say 'Drink Me.' So I should probably drink it."

Seriously? I shake my head. Didn't her parents teach her not to drink from random bottles?

Then again, we've been eating and drinking random stuff all day.

Frankie, Robin, Penny, and I watch as Alice takes a sip from the bottle.

"Ahhh!" she cries as her entire body starts shrinking. "Why am I getting smaller?" She's suddenly a foot high like we are.

Frankie squeals with excitement.

"Oh! I didn't know anyone else was here!" Alice says, noticing Frankie. Then she sees me, Robin, and Penny. Then the two rabbits. I guess we're interrupting her story after all.

"How curious!" Alice exclaims, glancing down at herself and her itty-bitty blue dress.

I see her look up at the giant table. I can tell she's confused.

I'm about to tell her about the magic potion she drank, when Robin rushes over and gives Alice a big hug. Well, a tiny hug.

Robin's face is flushed. "Alice! Alice! It's you! Oh my goodness, oh my goodness. This is amazing. It's you! It's really you! Alice!"

"What? You know me?" Alice asks, stepping back and looking even more confused.

"Of course we know you," Frankie says breathlessly. She bites her thumbnail, looking a little shy again. "You're Alice."

"Well, I don't know how you could possibly know that," Alice responds, her hands on her hips. "We've never met."

"We just did," Robin says, jumping and clapping her hands the way she does when she's super excited.

"This place is getting curiouser and curiouser!" Alice says.

And she just got here. Wait till she takes a stroll around the rest of Wonderland.

"Could I have your autograph?" Robin asks. "Please, please, please? I forgot my autograph book at home, but maybe you could sign a piece of paper for me?"

Alice takes another step back from Robin, alarm in her eyes. "So sorry," she says. "But I can't help you."

"You can write on our arms," Frankie offers. "Do you have a pen?"

"I have a pencil in my pocket," Penny says, reaching into her jeans. "But it won't write on skin. I so wish I had my sketch pad." She's gazing, mesmerized, at Alice, just like Robin and Frankie are.

Alice is looking at the three of them as if they've lost their minds.

"I love your dress," Robin gushes to Alice.

"I love your dress, too," Penny says. "And your hair. We're practically hair twins! Maybe we can form a Blond Hair Club."

I roll my eyes. This is a little embarrassing. I mean, it IS very cool to meet the real Alice. And sure, my friends are new to this. But I've met a lot of fictional characters before.

There's no way I was this awestruck when I met Snow White. No way.

Was I?

Maybe.

Alice frowns. "I'm afraid I don't understand."

"Sorry." I finally speak up, and step forward. "They're just excited to meet you. I'm Abby, and the redhead is Robin, the girl with the glasses is Frankie, and the other blonde is Penny. And you already know the White Rabbit. Or at least one of them."

Alice looks at the rabbit who fell in before her. "Well, I wouldn't say I KNOW the White Rabbit. But I heard him saying he was late for something. I'd never seen a talking rabbit before. So I followed him. And fell down the hole." Then she looks at the *other* White Rabbit. "There are two of you?"

Yes, but only one is the REAL White Rabbit. The other is someone in disguise. And I'm going to figure out which is which.

Somehow.

The rabbit who fell in right before Alice is glaring at the other rabbit. "Why are you wearing my clothes and pretending to be me?" he demands.

"I have no idea what you're talking about!" the rabbit sitting on the table says. "I'm just me!"

"Pretending to be ME!" the rabbit standing near Alice says.

Wait a minute.

I know which is the REAL White Rabbit.

The rabbit who was sitting on the glass table when my friends and I came in has to be the FAKE rabbit. Because Alice follows the REAL rabbit down the rabbit hole. It's her story, after all.

"You're the fake rabbit!" I say, pointing to the impostor rabbit on the table. "You're the one who tricked us into eating the queen's tarts so we'd get in trouble!"

"Are you sure about that, Abby?" Robin asks me worriedly.

"I'm sure," I say, still glaring at the fake rabbit. "So why are you in disguise? Who are you really?"

The fake rabbit sticks out his pink tongue at me. Real mature.

Except he's not quite the same as he was a moment ago. He's getting slightly bigger, for one. His white fur disappears. His floppy ears disappear. He's transforming from a rabbit — into a person. Suddenly, he's a short, skinny man with a big head and a long, narrow nose. His face is an orange-peach color and his teeth are pearly white.

Oh, wow. Oh, no.

"Ah, back to myself," the little man says, scratching his arm. "Being a rabbit gets itchy and hot. And carrots are disgusting. Blech. I am never eating another carrot again."

"Uh . . . um . . . what *are* you?" Penny says.

"I have a better question," I say. "*Who* are you?"

He glares at me. "I'm Gluck."

"Gluck?" Penny says. "What kind of name is that?"

"It's the kind of name evil fairies have!" Gluck yells.

I shiver. No. No. No. I hate evil fairies! Why do stories always have evil fairies?

"But . . . but . . . but . . ."

Gluck narrows his beady eyes at me. He pulls a tiny walkie-talkie from his coat pocket. "Guards! The thieves are in the hallway! Hurry!"

ACK.

Before we can even think about running and hiding, one of the blue doors bursts open.

All of a sudden, five cards storm the hallway. Oh no oh no. It's the Three of Clubs and her henchmen.

I glance back at Gluck.

He smirks right at me, looking very pleased. "Gotcha," he says. "Now you're trapped!"

"But why?" I ask. "Why are you trying to trap me?"

"You know why," he says.

Huh? "I don't know why!"

He smirks again, and then POOF — he disappears.

"There are the thieves!" the Three of Clubs shouts, hitting her club against her palm. "Apprehend them at once!"

"NO!" I yell. The Five of Clubs grabs my arm.

The Six of Clubs grabs Penny.

The Seven of Clubs grabs Frankie.

The Eight of Clubs grabs Robin.

The Nine of Clubs grabs Alice.

"You five girls are under arrest for stealing the queen's tarts!" the Three of Clubs announces.

"But that's not fair!" Penny cries. "They weren't even good! They were sour! And Frankie and Alice weren't even there!"

I slap my free hand against my forehead. Penny just admitted she ate a tart! In front of witnesses!

Frankie kicks at her guard. "Take that, you piece of cardboard!"

Go, Frankie.

"Off with her head for sure," the Seven of Clubs growls as he rubs his shin.

"What are you going to do with us?" Penny asks. "I demand to know!"

"Oh dear oh my oh goodness," says the real White Rabbit, hopping about worriedly.

"Prisoners aren't allowed to make demands, so shush!" the Eight of Clubs bellows at Penny.

"Let go of me!" Alice says to the card who is gripping her by the arm. "I haven't stolen anything! I just got here!"

"Sure you did," the Three of Clubs says. "You are a little girl like the others — you are probably in cahoots."

"Cahoots bashmoots!" Alice yells. "This can't be happening! Dinah! Dinah! Where is Dinah! Attack the cards, Dinah, attack!"

Who's Dinah?

"You're coming with us," the Three of Clubs says. "All five of you tart stealers will be put on trial immediately."

The cards pull us toward the small door. Noooo!

"Oh dear oh goodness oh dear," the real White Rabbit says again, watching us go.

"I am sorry we ruined your dream," Frankie says to Alice as we're all dragged outside.

Alice tilts her head. "This is a dream?"

"No," I say. "This is a nightmare."

chapter fourteen

The Queen of Mean

Waiting for us outside the door is a horse-drawn carriage with bars all around it. The cards throw me, Penny, Robin, Frankie, and Alice into the back of the carriage and lock the door.

Frankie wraps her hands around the bars. "Let us out right now!" she demands.

"Yeah!" Robin says.

"Can't we work out a deal?" Penny adds. "My parents are rich! Just name your price!"

The Three of Clubs narrows her dark eyes at us. "I've been looking for you thieves all afternoon. Now I've caught you. I don't need *your* money. The queen will reward me."

With a jolt, the carriage starts moving.

"At least we're sitting down," Frankie says, taking off her glasses and rubbing her eyes. "I'm kind of exhausted."

My heart is pounding. This is terrible. "We need a *plan*," I insist as we bounce along the road. "What's our plan?"

"I don't know!" Penny cries.

"I wish someone would explain what's going on," Alice moans.

"Sorry, Alice," Robin tells her. "But look on the bright side. This way we can get to know each other! Tell me about yourself. Do you have a BFF?"

"What is a BFF?" Alice asks.

"BFF!" Robin repeats. "A Best Friend Forever? Don't you have a BFF?"

Alice thinks about that. "Well, I am sort of close with my sister. And my cat, Dinah. But no, I guess I don't have a Best Friend Forever."

Aha. Dinah is her cat.

"You can be BFFs with *me*," Penny says. Then she gives me a look. "We can even make necklaces. PA necklaces. For Penny and Alice."

I feel Penny's eyes burning into me as she says it. I finger my FRA necklace. FRA, for Frankie, Robin, Abby.

Robin is touching her own FRA necklace. Frankie runs her fingers over her FRA necklace, too.

It never occurred to me that our necklaces would make Penny feel left out. It never occurred to me that Penny even noticed our necklaces.

"I think we have bigger things to worry about than necklaces," Alice points out.

It's true. The carriage goes over a big bump on the path, and then finally comes to a stop. The Three of Clubs unlocks the door and yanks us out. The cards march us to the castle.

I've been to a lot of castles in my time. But this one . . . this one . . .

It's really *all* red. Is it made out of . . . candy hearts? I look more closely. It is! Except these candy hearts don't have sayings on them like the ones we get on Valentine's Day. I wonder if we're supposed to eat one of the hearts to get home. I'm thinking about investigating this, when the card holding my arm gives me a shove.

"Into the castle," he commands.

We're ushered inside the main hall. It has white walls, a checkerboard floor, and a checkerboard ceiling. I'm getting dizzy.

And then I see them at the front of the room.

The king and queen!

Frankie immediately curtsies.

Oh. Right. I do the same.

Robin and Penny follow suit.

The queen is also a playing card. She is, of course, the Queen of Hearts. And she's sitting on a big red throne. She has a heart-shaped face, and her dark hair is streaked with gray and coiled up in a bun. A gold crown dotted with jewels sits on top of the bun. She's wearing a purple velvet robe around her card body and very high-heeled purple velvet shoes. She's much older than I was expecting. She looks like she's in her seventies, at least. Beside her, on a gold throne, is the King of Hearts. He's also a card. His crown is smaller than his head. He's also old.

"I didn't know there was a king in this story," I whisper to Frankie.

"There is," she says. "But it's clear who the real ruler is."

Rows and rows of gold chairs are set up facing the queen and king. All the cards and animals of Wonderland are in the chairs, even the mouse and the duck and the rat and the birds. I see the Duchess holding the piglet in the little yellow blanket. And the fuzzy green caterpillar, who's still smoking his pipe.

Smoking is allowed in here? Smoking and peanut butter? Aren't there any rules here at all?

The cards drag us down the aisle to the front of the room. I see the Cheshire Cat resting on a side table. Sitting right in the front row are the Mad Hatter and the March Hare, with the little Dormouse sleeping on top of the Hatter's hat. The angry orange birds squawk as we pass them. But the nice birds — the duck and rainbow parrots and the pink robin and the pretty blue-and-white bird — smile at us.

"We're rooting for you," the mouse whispers.

"Go, Team Girls!" says the blue-and-white bird.

Cliff is there, too. He's sitting beside the Duchess. And making a peace sign with his fingers. Poor Cliff. I wonder why he always hangs out with the Duchess. Maybe he has nowhere else to go.

There's a long table set up facing the king and queen. The cards march us over and tell us to sit down at the table. I'm in the middle, with Penny on my left and Alice on my right, and Robin and Frankie on either end.

A guard-card is posted at each side of our table. So much for trying to escape.

The Three of Clubs stands to the side of the queen and king. "The court is now called to order!" she bellows.

The court. The court! THE COURT!

OMG, I'm in court! How cool is that?

I jump in my seat. Penny glares at me for being excited. I can't help it, though. I've never seen a REAL trial before. I have always wanted to see a real trial.

I have always wanted to be the *judge* at a real trial. I guess I just never expected to be the one ON trial.

"The trial begins!" the Three of Clubs announces.

Alice shifts nervously in the seat beside me.

I feel bad that Alice got mixed up in this. She was sup-posed to meet all these wacky Wonderland creatures and have all these adventures and now her story is ending right at the beginning.

Unless . . . well, in the original story she wakes up when she's in the courtroom, right?

But what if, now that we messed the story up, Alice doesn't wake up in the courtroom scene? I shiver. What if she never wakes up? What if she's stuck here forever?

We have to save her.

"Read the accusations against the thieves," the king says.

The Three of Clubs clears her throat, then pulls a trumpet from her pocket. She blows the trumpet three times and puts it away.

"The Queen of Hearts, she made some tarts, all on a summer's day," she says. "The girls have no hearts, they stole those tarts, and munched them all away!"

Yup, we definitely changed the story.

A collective gasp rises in the courtroom. Everyone is whispering and pointing at us. My cheeks burn.

"These five girls — Abby, Frankie, Robin, Penny, and Alice — are thieves!" the Three of Clubs continues. "They have been stealing food and drink from Wonderland all day long. I saw them stealing the queen's tarts with my own two eyes!"

"Terrible!" the Mad Hatter clucks.

"It's true," I hear the Duchess say, covering the piglet-baby's ears. "They spilled my soup! To think I invited them into my home!"

We did not spill her soup! Lick it, yes; spill it, no.

"Snake thieves!" the orange bird calls out. "They tried to eat my eggs!"

"Silence in the court!" the Queen of Hearts bellows. "I can't hear myself think! What was I thinking about, dear?" she asks the king.

"Was it what I was thinking?" the king says.

"Maybe," the queen responds. "Were you thinking that these five girls look very guilty?"

The king nods. "I don't remember."

"I'm not guilty!" Alice cries. "I didn't eat anything! Honestly, I'm quite hungry. Did you say something about tarts?"

"They weren't even good," Penny says, wrinkling her nose.

"Insolence!" the Three of Clubs shouts at Penny. "When you are found guilty, you will have your head chopped off twice!"

Robin's eyes widen. "*When* we're found guilty?"

"HUSH!" the Queen of Hearts shouts. "Or it'll be off with your head!"

I have to do something.

I take a deep breath. I can do this. It's a trial, after all. And I want to be a lawyer, right? Well, a judge, but a lawyer first.

I've been preparing for this my whole life.

"Excuse me?" I say and stand up. "The point of a trial is to find out if the accused person is guilty. And, um, since anything is allowed in this court, I am hereby announcing myself as lawyer for the defense." I look at my friends. "That's us," I whisper.

"Fine. Whatever," the queen says to me, waving her hand dismissively. She turns to the Three of Clubs. "Call your first witness."

"I call the Hatter to the stand!" the Three of Clubs says.

The Mad Hatter strolls up to the chair that's set up beside the two thrones.

"Hatter," the Three of Clubs says. "Do you swear to tell the truth, the whole truth, and nothing BUT the truth?"

"I will tell nothing of the truth," the Mad Hatter says.

Wait. That didn't sound right.

"Objection!" I call out. "He said he would tell nothing of the truth!"

"Perhaps," the Mad Hatter says. "But aren't there many truths?"

"No," I say. "There is only one truth."

"If you say so," he says. "But I say differently."

"Objection overruled," the queen says. "Please continue."

"Excellent," the Three of Clubs responds. "Hatter, did you witness these girls steal food or a beverage from your tea party?"

The Mad Hatter jumps out of his seat. "Is it tea time already? Why, I believe it is." The Hatter marches toward the door. The March Hare, carrying the Dormouse in his hand, is right behind him.

"Witness, come back here this instant, or it's off with your head!" the queen shouts.

The Hatter freezes and turns back. He walks to the chair. He adjusts his hat and sits down. "Make it fast!" He looks at his watch. "It's six o'clock."

The Three of Clubs glares at the Hatter and repeats her question. "Did you witness these girls steal anything from the tea party?"

"Those girls?" the Mad Hatter says, pointing at us.

The Three of Clubs looks very frustrated. She stomps her foot. "Yes! Those girls!"

The Mad Hatter scratches his chin. "They were invited guests at my tea party. Invited. Guests. So how could they have stolen anything?"

Hah!

"But —" the Three of Clubs begins.

"The witness has spoken!" I yell. "He's spoken! We didn't steal anything! We were his guests! Case dismissed!"

I high-five Penny and Robin and Frankie. I try to high-five Alice, but she tilts her head and doesn't know what to do. She's clearly never high-fived before.

"Not quite," the Queen of Hearts says. "Next witness."

"I call the White Rabbit," the Three of Clubs announces.

Penny and I both gasp. WHICH White Rabbit will it be? I look over to the chairs. I only see one White Rabbit. He's wearing his red coat and little round eyeglasses. But what if it's Gluck, the evil fairy? What if he transformed back into a rabbit after he disappeared from the hallway?

The White Rabbit pulls out his pocket watch, checks the

time, and then hurries to the witness chair. I crane my neck to see the time on his watch.

It says six o'clock. Why am I not surprised?

I wring my hands. If only I knew the time back in Smithville. I hope my parents haven't come to pick me up from Penny's yet.

The Three of Clubs clears her throat. "Mr. White Rabbit, do you swear to tell the truth, the whole truth, and nothing but the truth?"

"I do," the rabbit says. "But you must hurry! I'll be late!"

"What could possibly be more important than a trial?" the Three of Clubs yells.

"Off with his head!" the queen shouts.

"Dear, let the rabbit give his testimony," the king says.

"What is testimony?" Alice whispers to me.

"It's what a witness says happened," I whisper back.

"White Rabbit," the Three of Clubs begins. "Have you seen the girls drink or eat anything that does not belong to them?"

"Well —" he begins.

I hold my breath.

"Actually, no, ma'am," the White Rabbit answers.

The courtroom erupts. Everyone is murmuring.

"May I remind you that you must tell the truth!" the Three of Clubs snaps.

"I am telling the truth, ma'am," says the rabbit. "I saw the girls increase in size. And I believe they did some damage to my windows and possibly my chimney. But I did not actually SEE the girls drink anything."

"That's right!" Frankie whispers to me. "He was sleeping in his bedroom when we drank the potion, remember?"

Yay! This means it's the real White Rabbit in the witness chair.

"I am, however, told they ate my cake," he says.

"Objection!" I call out, jumping back up. "Didn't your children throw the cake at our mouths? So doesn't that mean they gave it to us?"

He nods. "Yes. I suppose they did."

Ha! I'm good at this. I am going to be the best lawyer ever. "So we didn't steal it, then! Case dismissed!" I yell.

"I don't think so," the Three of Clubs says. "I believe you saw at least one of the girls drink the shrinking potion. Correct, rabbit?"

He nods. "That's right. I did. I saw Alice drink it. When she first got here."

Oh, no.

Murmurs spread through the room.

Alice pales and shrinks back in her chair.

"But . . . but . . . there was a sign on it!" I say. "It said 'Drink Me'! That was an invitation! It can't be considered a crime to drink something that instructs one to drink it, can it?"

"She makes a good point," the king says, his forehead wrinkling.

The White Rabbit looks at his pocket watch. "Oh dear oh dear, I'm very late. May I be excused now?"

"Yes," the Three of Clubs says. "As long as you have nothing else to testify about?"

"I do not." He jumps off the chair and hops out of the courtroom.

"Next up is the caterpillar!" says the Three of Clubs.

The caterpillar? Are they going to get everyone we've ever spoken with to testify against us?

The caterpillar scoots his way toward the front. He sits down and blows a smoke ring right in the Three of Clubs's face.

"I heard the girls ate both sides of your mushroom," the Three of Clubs says.

"He told us to!" I say.

The caterpillar nods. He blows another smoke ring. "Both true," he drawls.

"See? See?" I call out. "This is ridiculous! No one has anything on us! There's no proof of a crime. So please let us go!"

The queen nods. "If no one can prove that they stole my tarts —"

"I can," says a deep voice.

We turn around.

It's Gluck. The evil fairy. In his human form.

Noooooo.

"He doesn't have any evidence!" I cry.

"Au contraire," Gluck says, walking past us. "I have photographic evidence."

And then he lifts up Robin's pink sparkle cell phone and smiles.

chapter fifteen

The Verdict

my phone!" Robin cries. "I want that back!"

"I'm sure you do," Gluck says and lets out his evil laugh. "But it has incriminating evidence."

"The selfies," Robin says, slumping into her seat.

"How many did you take?" I whisper.

"A lot," she says.

"What's a selfie?" Alice asks.

"It's . . . a picture," I say. "Of us. Eating the tarts."

"Oh, no!" she cries.

"That's not good," Frankie says, shaking her head.

"I can project them so everyone can see," Gluck says. He pulls a little silver clicker out of his pocket. The next thing I know, there are huge pictures projected up on the wall behind the queen. Pictures of me, Robin, and Penny munching on the tomato tarts.

"How did he do that?" Robin asks. "I don't even know how to do that! Is it in the Cloud?"

"He's a fairy," I say. "He can do anything he wants."

Gluck presses on the silver clicker and new pictures pop up. There's one of me standing in the garden, my mouth stuffed with tomato.

Great. Just great.

"See?" Gluck says. "They're guilty."

I jump up. "Okay, you got us. We'll admit that we ate the tarts. But! We only ate them because Gluck told us to! We would never have eaten the tarts if we'd known they were yours!" I tell the queen.

"She's lying!" Gluck yells.

"*You're* lying!" I yell back.

"Well," the king begins. "I hereby declare —"

"I'm the declarer!" the queen says. "I hereby declare that I will take the new evidence into consideration before I find you guilty."

That doesn't sound good.

"Order in the court," the Three of Clubs shouts. "One-minute recess!"

Order? What order? This place has order? Could have fooled me.

Frankie, Robin, Penny, Alice, and I remain seated. We could try to make a run for it, but there are still those two guards posted on both sides of our table.

I glance over at Frankie. She's deep in thought, probably trying to remember what happens next. Or what's supposed to happen in the book, at least. Even Robin looks worried. Alice is sitting straight in her chair, her hands folded, with a perplexed expression on her face. And Penny — huh. She's not exactly shaking in her sneakers. In fact, she's doing what she does when she's bored in class. Doodling on the desk with her pencil.

Except, I have to say, this is more than a doodle. She's drawing a really good picture of the Queen and King of Hearts.

The Three of Clubs glares at Penny. "Now the thief is defacing the property of the court!" she yells. "She dares draw the likeness of the king and queen!"

The King of Hearts gasps. "What! Only the royal artist can draw our likeness!"

"Let me see that!" the queen shouts. She scoots off her throne, marches down to our table, and comes around to our side.

Penny smiles at her. "I don't think I got your pretty hair just right, but I don't have my good pastels with me."

The queen looks at the drawing. She narrows her beady eyes and lifts her chin. "I do have pretty hair, don't I?" the queen says. "And what lovely expression. My child, I'm impressed."

Penny looks at me and smiles. Then she looks back up at the queen and bats her eyelashes. "Do you think you could spare my head? And my friends'? Robin's my BFF. Frankie is very smart and helps me with book reports. Abby can be bossy, but that made her a really good lawyer, don't you think? You never know when YOU might be on trial, Your Majesty. Oh, and Alice didn't even get to see Wonderland yet."

The queen stares at Penny. "Why would *I* ever be on trial?" She laughs for a good two minutes. "You've amused me. But I shall think about your request. Court is in recess for one more minute!"

The queen rushes back to her throne. She and the king start whispering to each other. I lean forward, trying to hear. Lots of whispers. The queen stomps her foot. The king stomps his. The queen lifts her chin and smiles meanly.

The Three of Clubs sounds the trumpet. "The queen has come to a decision!"

I glance at Penny and Robin on my left. Alice and Frankie on my right.

"You will now be sentenced," the queen says.

"As attorney for the defense, I must remind you that we haven't been found guilty!" I say.

"SILENCE!" the king shouts. "The queen has spoken!"

"Indeed I have," the queen says. "Off with their heads!"

"What?" I cry. "No! I object! OBJECTION! I did a great job! I did not lose this case!"

"You did do a great job, Abby," Robin tells me. "I wouldn't take it personally."

"However —" the queen continues. "Everyone wait, I'm about to sneeze!"

The queen sneezes. Her cardboard body flutters. "As I was saying. The young artist will be spared. I am impressed with her talent, and would like her to come be my heir. But the other four girls ARE GUILTY AS CHARGED!"

Huh? What? "NO!" I shout.

"I'm not guilty!" Alice cries. "I just got here! I wasn't even in their pictures!"

"SILENCE!" the king bellows.

Penny looks shocked. "Be your heir?" she gasps. "You want me to stay here with you?"

The queen nods. "Yes. The king and I have no heir, and we have been looking to groom someone to take over the kingdom. You are a good fit."

"Excuse me? M'lady?" asks the Three of Clubs. "Wouldn't you be better off choosing a card? Someone who shares your DNA perhaps?" She stands up straight. "Perhaps a club?"

"I can choose whoever I want to choose," the queen snarls. "And I want the girl with the pretty hair to be my heir!"

"What about an actual hare?" the king says. "They make great heirs, too."

"Swallow," Robin says.

"Huh?" I say, turning to her.

"Swallow," she says slowly. "What if the Cheshire Cat meant something else? The way words have different meanings. Like heir and hare. Or feet and feet."

Frankie's eyes widen. She gasps and points to one of the birds. "Swallow!"

Are they losing it? They're not going to try and eat one of the birds, are they?

"Isn't a swallow a type of bird?" Robin asks Frankie.

"Yes!" Frankie exclaims. "It is! The blue-and-white bird! It's called a swallow! That's what I was trying to remember. It's been driving me crazy!"

It's called a swallow? There's a type of bird called a swallow?

A swallow taken will bring you back.

I draw in a deep breath. "Are you saying that the 'swallow taken' isn't something to eat? Or drink?" I ask. "That instead it's a, a —"

"Kind of bird!" Robin, Frankie, and I say at the same time.

Oh my goodness.

I glance over at where the Cheshire Cat is sitting. He looks at me, grins, and gives me a thumbs-up. Make that a paws-up. Then he disappears.

Yup.

It's the bird. The bird is going to take us home.

"Hey!" I call out. "Come here, swallow!"

The bird dives toward us. Before anyone knows what's happening, I climb on his back. Since I'm still tiny, I fit on easily. "Come on, guys!" I call to my friends. "Let's go!"

Robin and Frankie immediately jump on behind me.

"Penny, let's go!" I say.

Penny hesitates. "But . . . but . . . No."

"No?" I repeat. "What are you talking about? Penny, we have to leave. Now. Get on the swallow."

Penny narrows her eyes. "I am so sick of you telling me what to do! You are NOT the boss of me!"

Is she kidding me right now? "Excuse me? I'm trying to save you!"

"I don't need your help," she says. "I can save myself. And maybe I don't want to leave."

Huh? "But you hate Wonderland. Remember? It makes no sense."

"The queen likes me! She wants to be with me!" She looks sadly at the ground. "That's more than I can say about anyone in Smithville."

"What are you talking about?" I ask.

"My parents are never there," she says. "Sheila only takes care of me because it's her job. I bet she hasn't even noticed I'm gone. And you guys . . . well, you guys have each other! Robin is supposed to be my best friend, but we all know she's really your best friend. She barely even talked to me today. If I stay here, no one will even miss me. And the queen kind of looks like my grandma."

"Your grandma looked like a card?" Robin asks.

"Of course not," Penny says. "But they have the same heart-shaped face and dark gray bun."

Aw. Poor Penny.

"You will make an excellent princess," the queen tells Penny, pursing her lips. "Come along, dear. Let me show you Wonderland. Would you like a tart? I don't just have tomato. I have asparagus, too!"

"Penny, no," Robin rushes to say. "I'm sorry if I didn't talk to you enough today, but you *are* one of my best friends. And I want you to come home."

"We *need* you to come home," Frankie says.

"Nobody needs me for anything," Penny says sadly.

"We need you," I insist, meaning it. "You helped! That portrait you drew was amazing! You and I both agree that rules are good. We have that in common, right? And without you, we don't have our P!"

"Huh?"

"Our P!" I say. "In our FRAP necklace! Who's going to be our P?"

She cracks a smile. "Really?"

"Really! Now get on the swallow," I order. "Pretty please with a mushroom on top?"

She smiles again. And then finally, Penny climbs on behind us.

"No!" the queen hollers. "Come back with my heir!"

"I can't be your heir," Penny says. "I'm sorry."

Cliff stands up. "I'll be your heir!" he calls out.

The queen eyes him up and down. "You?"

"A son!" the king cries. "I have always wanted a son."

"I thought you wanted to get out of Wonderland?" I ask Cliff.

"I don't mind staying," he tells me. "It's kind of groovy. As long as you're going back to help her."

"To help who?" I ask him. "What do you mean?"

"Do you have a talent?" the queen asks Cliff.

"I can dance," he says, swinging his hips. "Do you know how to disco?"

"Okay, swallow," I say to the bird. "We're ready."

"What about Alice?" Robin asks.

Oh, no. What about Alice? Should we bring her back with us? No. We can't take her to modern-day Smithville. She needs to return to her sister and Dinah.

I look over at Alice, who's sitting at the table with her chin in her hands.

"I know. We should pinch her," Robin says. "That will wake her up!"

"Good idea," Penny says.

Robin jumps off the swallow and pinches Alice's arm hard, leaving a red mark.

"Ouch!" Alice cries. "What did you do that for?"

"I was trying to wake you," Robin says. "But I guess it is a myth."

"Told you," I say.

"She'll be fine," Frankie says. "Don't worry. She'll wake up soon anyway."

"But what if she doesn't?" I ask, biting my lip. "What if she's stuck here forever?"

"I agree with Frankie," Penny says. "She's going to wake up when she's ready."

"But . . ." My voice trails off.

Frankie puts her hand on my shoulder. "I know you've done this before. And you're the expert. But you can trust us on this. Okay?"

I nod. "Okay."

"Come on, Robin!" Penny calls.

"One sec," Robin says. She leans over to grab her cell phone off the evidence desk and then jumps back on the swallow. "Got it! I can't leave this behind!"

And with that, the swallow takes off.

"Good-bye, Alice!" we shout, waving, as we rise into the air.

"Good-bye!" she calls out. "It was nice to meet you, BFFs!"

Aw.

"Should we go after them, m'lady?" the Three of Clubs asks the queen.

"Give them a fifty-two-second head start and then chase them down," the queen says.

Yikes. "Go, go, go!" I say to the swallow. "Can you take us to the hallway with all the doors and up through the rabbit hole?" I ask.

The swallow nods and soars away.

We zoom out of the castle and over to the metal blue door. The swallow stops short, and I jump off his back to open the door.

"Let's go!" I cry, getting back on the bird in front of Penny.

"Hang on!" the swallow says.

The bird flies through the doorway and then down through the hallway of doors.

"STOP THAT SWALLOW!" I hear the Three of Clubs shout from outside.

Oh, no! The cards! Our fifty-two-second lead must be up.

The door behind us bursts open and the entire deck of cards is chasing down the hallway after us. Well, minus the Queen and King of Hearts.

Ahhh!

"Faster, Mr. Swallow!" I cry.

The swallow looks up to the bottom of the rabbit hole. "Hold on, girls. There's lots of furniture flying around up there. And going up through the ground might hurt."

"He's not going to push his way through, is he?" Penny asks, cringing.

But the swallow isn't moving at all. He's just flying low at the bottom of the rabbit hole.

"Something is on my leg!" the swallow cries.

"What?" I say. I look down. Ahh!

It's Gluck!

He's lassoed the swallow's foot with a rope! He's holding it tightly.

"Try to fly!" Frankie cries.

"I can't," the swallow says. "His grip is too strong!"

I try to kick at Gluck, but I can't reach him.

"You're going to be trapped here forever," the evil fairy says to me. "Mwahaha! You'll never be able to save Maryrose!"

Oh. OH.

Gluck is trying to trap me here because of Maryrose! He doesn't want me to help her!

"Are you the evil fairy who cursed her?" I ask.

"I helped!" he cries. "And I'm helping now!"

He's holding on to the rope with a steel grip. The poor swallow is trying to fly up but can't.

"Let go!" I yell down at Gluck.

"Never!"

Robin takes out her cell phone.

Is it really the time for a selfie?

The next thing I know, Robin throws the phone at Gluck's head.

"Ouch!" he cries, letting go of the swallow and cradling his nose with both hands.

"Good-bye, phone!" Robin cries, watching it fall to the ground in Wonderland.

"I'm free!" the swallow says, flapping his wings.

"THANK YOU, ROBIN!" I cry as the bird soars up.

We all hold tight to his feathers.

We pass the flying loaf of bread and the jar of mayonnaise. The ketchup floats toward us.

"Eat the ketchup!" the swallow calls out.

"Really?" Penny shouts back.

"Yes!" the swallow shouts. "It will bring you back to normal size!"

Wait until Jonah hears about this. I grab the bottle of ketchup and squirt some in my mouth. Suddenly, my hands are getting bigger! My legs are getting longer. I'm growing back to my original size! I hand the bottle to Penny and she squirts some in her mouth. Frankie and Robin do the same.

"Don't forget *me*!" the swallow cries, and Robin squirts some ketchup in his mouth, too.

Soon, Penny, Frankie, and Robin are growing alongside me. Before I know it —

We're all regular size again! And the swallow is extra-big, so we all fit comfortably. Hurrah!

A bookshelf goes swirling past us on our way up. And a bed. There's the kitchen. There's that polka-dot umbrella again. And a rocking chair. Good-bye, weird Wonderland. I will miss you.

A shelf floats overhead.

"Ooh, an egg salad sandwich," Robin says, reaching for one and popping it in her mouth.

"Watch out!" I say, but it's too late.

When Robin took the egg sandwich, the shelf tilted and now a container of what looks like baby powder is sprinkling over our heads. The powder lands mostly on Robin, a little on Frankie, and a tiny bit sprinkles on Penny. It just barely misses me.

It smells like . . . like . . . I can't place it. Oh! It smells like watermelon. Ha.

"What *was* that?" I ask.

No one answers.

"Guys?" I turn back and see that Frankie, Robin, and Penny's eyes are closed.

Are they sleeping?

I think they are!

The baby powder put them to sleep!

The swallow continues to fly up and up and up, and even though my friends are asleep, it's like they're seat-belted in.

Finally, the swallow bursts up through the ground. We're out of the rabbit hole and back on the golf course!

"Do you know where Penny lives?" I ask the swallow. "Just over the fence and through those trees."

The swallow flies over the fence and into Penny's backyard. Luckily, I don't see Sheila the nanny anywhere.

"You can put us on the patio," I say. "That's where we were playing cards before."

"Will do," the swallow says. He gently lowers his back and turns slightly so that each girl lands right on a chair.

"Thank you, swallow," I say. "You saved us!"

"My pleasure," the swallow says, and then flies away. I watch him soar through the trees toward the golf course.

I'm home! Wahoo! Well, I'm in Smithville, anyway. I look through the sliding glass doors to the family room of Penny's house and can see the clock on the wall.

It's not six o'clock! It's only one! Hardly any time has passed at all.

WHEW.

Frankie, Robin, and Penny each let out a snore and turn over onto their sides.

I let out a huge sigh of relief. We're in Smithville. Everything is back to normal.

Except for the fact that there's an evil fairy out there who maybe wants to trap me.

I wonder what happened to Gluck after we left. Did he turn to dust? Become a puddle of fairy goo? Is he stuck in Wonderland? Or is he somewhere out here in the real world?

I shiver.

Because if he can disguise himself, I won't recognize him in the future.

Or know when I might see him again.

chapter sixteen

Home Sweet Home

While I'm waiting for Frankie, Robin, and Penny to wake up, I think about how I'm going to handle the fact that THEY KNOW. They know I go into stories. They know an evil fairy is after me.

I guess I'll just have to see how the conversation goes when they wake up. Right now, thinking about it is giving me a headache, so I go inside the house. Sheila is sitting in the family room, watching a reality TV show. She doesn't even notice me. I can see what Penny is talking about. It has to be lonely around here.

I head upstairs to Penny's room.

I look at Penny's trophies. And her old stuffed animals. And her one book. Her fancy copy of *Alice's Adventures in Wonderland*.

The copy her grandmother gave her. The grandmother she seems to miss a lot.

I learned a lot about Penny in Wonderland. She's so much more than I thought she was.

I guess everyone is. Even Frankie and Robin have more to them than I ever knew.

I carefully take the book off the shelf. The cover is leather and has a big swirled A for *Alice* and W for *Wonderland*, with an illustration of Alice. She looks just like she did when we met her.

I open it to the beginning. Looks normal. I keep turning the pages, and then I get to the part when Alice falls down the hole:

"Down she came upon a heap of sticks and dry leaves, and the fall was over. Alice was not a bit hurt, and she jumped up on to her feet in a moment . . ."

I blink and read what's next:

"In front of her were four tiny . . . what were they? Mice? No. They looked like little girls! Why did this place have tiny little girls?"

Oh, wow. Oh, no. I'm almost positive that's not in the original story. Which means . . .

We're in the book! We're in *Alice's Adventures in Wonderland*! And on the next page, there's an illustration! Of a tiny me, tiny Frankie, tiny Robin, and tiny Penny! I can't believe it. I've never seen myself in a book before.

I flip ahead a few more pages to see what else might have changed.

Cliff was adopted by the king and queen and he's turned Wonderland into a disco?

The Mad Hatter wins a dance competition?

What is going on?

I flip to the last page. Alice wakes up from her dream. She's sitting beside a tree with her sister.

Whew.

My friends were right. Alice really does wake up on her own and she's okay.

All's well that ends well.

Still, Gluck is out there somewhere. I need to talk to Maryrose.

But first, I have to make sure my friends agree to keep this OUR secret. Will they? I know I can count on Frankie and Robin. But what about Penny?

I put the book back on the shelf. I rush outside and find the three of them still sleeping at the patio table. But a few minutes later, I hear a big yawn. Robin is waking up. Frankie and Penny are both still asleep.

"Wow," Robin says. "Did I fall asleep?"

"Yes," I say slowly. "You did."

"Weird," she says, looking confused. "Are we still playing crazy eights?"

Really? Nothing about Wonderland at all? Does that mean what I think it means? Does she not remember? Did the baby powder make her forget?

Robin blinks. And blinks again. She looks at the table. "Where's my phone?"

Last time I saw it, it was flying through the air and hitting Gluck in the nose. I don't say this. I don't say anything. Instead, I shrug.

Penny sits up and stretches. She tightens her ponytail. She looks around the table.

Frankie shifts in her seat, also waking up. She rubs her eyes behind her glasses. "I had the craziest dream," she says.

I freeze.

"Tell us about it," Penny says. "Was I in it?"

Frankie nods. "You were. You all were."

Uh-oh. "What happened?" I ask.

"Well, we were playing cards in the backyard. And then we fell into *Alice's Adventures in Wonderland*!"

"Really?" Penny asks. "You dreamt about *Alice in Wonderland*?"

Phew. Penny doesn't seem to remember.

"I've always wanted to meet Alice," Robin says.

So Robin and Penny didn't dream it, then? Only Frankie did?

But she didn't *dream* it, of course. She lived it.

"*Alice* is one of my all-time favorite books," Frankie says. "Have any of you read it?"

"Of course I have," Penny says smugly.

Puh-lease.

But at least things are really back to normal.

"Can we go inside now?" I ask.

"Yeah," Robin says. "I'm cold."

"I'm changing the schedule up," Penny says. "I think we should make jewelry."

"Yeah?" Frankie asks. "What kind?"

"New necklaces. FRAP necklaces. They were Abby's idea."

Huh? "You . . . you . . . you . . . remember?"

Penny turns to me and smiles. "I remember *everything*."

My heart stops. Oh, no. But how? Why does Robin remember nothing, Frankie thinks she dreamed it, and Penny remembers everything?

I think back to the falling baby powder. Most of the powder fell on Robin. Then some fell on Frankie. Then hardly any fell on Penny. And none fell on me. That must be it. In fact, I can still see a bit of powder on Robin's nose, covering a freckle. So Robin doesn't have any memory of what happened, Frankie has half-memories that seem like dreams, and Penny . . .

Penny links her arm through mine. "Don't worry," she whispers. "Your secret is safe with me."

Penny knows!

"It is?" I whisper back. "Swear?"

"Yup," she says. "But maybe the necklaces can be PFRA? Or PARF? What do you think about PRAF? That's much better than FRAP."

Definitely back to normal. "I think that could be arranged," I say.

"Hey," Robin says, patting her pockets. "Guys? I really don't remember what I did with my phone."

Poor Robin.

"Are you guys ready for spaghetti with tomato sauce?" we hear Sheila ask from inside.

Frankie frowns. "Weirdly, I'm not that hungry."

"Me neither," says Robin, and lowers her voice. "And I'm not in the mood for anything with tomatoes."

Penny and I share a look and a smile.

When my parents pick me up, Jonah is already inside the car.

I give him a big kiss on the cheek. I missed having my brother in the story today.

"Don't slobber on me," he says.

I smile. "You will NEVER believe what happened," I whisper.

"What?" he asks.

"I'll tell you when we get home."

Back in his room, I tell Jonah everything. Falling down the hole into Wonderland. The magic potions. Being one foot tall. Then twelve feet tall. All the talking animals. The card-people. The flying ketchup. The two White Rabbits. And Gluck.

Prince barks like crazy, clearly jealous.

"No fair," Jonah says. "Flying ketchup! And you got to eat it!"

"Yeah," I say.

He lowers his voice. "Do you think Gluck is still out there?"

"I don't know," I say. I take the piece of mirror from my hoodie pocket. "Probably. I know it's not midnight but I'm going to fix the frame and try to tell Maryrose what happened. Coming?"

Jonah nods. "Of course."

Prince barks twice. Guess he's coming, too.

I stop by the kitchen for the superglue, and then Jonah, Prince, and I head downstairs and close the basement door behind us.

First I superglue the stone wand back into place on the frame. Perfect.

Then I knock on the mirror three times.

The glass starts rippling. Here comes Maryrose.

I see a fuzzy image of a woman's face with long wavy hair.

"You're back!" Maryrose says. "I'm so glad you're okay!"

"Does that mean you know what happened?" I ask. "You know that I went into *Alice's Adventures in Wonderland*?"

"I am aware," Maryrose says, clucking her tongue. "Gluck made the portal. He led you there, I'm afraid."

"He's that powerful?" I ask.

"Yes. But his power is somewhat limited. He was able to carry your card onto the golf course, and to replicate the rabbit hole, but he's not able to appear in the real world. I'm sorry. I tried to warn you. That was me shaking the piece of mirror frame in your pocket."

"It was?"

"Yes."

"Ah! I shouldn't have glued it back on, then!" I try to remove the piece, but it won't budge.

"Don't worry," she says. "My presence in the piece of frame only lasts for a short while. I could no longer communicate with you once you fell inside the story. I could see what was happening, but my hands were tied."

"Yikes," Jonah says.

"Do you know that Gluck tried to trap me so I couldn't help you?" I ask Maryrose. "He really has it in for you."

She nods. "I'm afraid so. Just as he wanted to keep Cliff from helping me over forty years ago. Cliff was close to saving me, just like you are. I would visit his mirror at night and Cliff would visit fairy tales. Until one day, he disappeared. I'm sorry I put you in danger," she says. "Once upon a time, a group of evil fairies cursed me, and now they are determined to do the same to anyone who comes to my aid."

I feel cold all over. Beside me, Jonah shivers.

"I'm sorry I couldn't help you in Wonderland," Maryrose goes on. "I didn't realize Gluck was responsible for Cliff's disappearance until today. I never expected that an evil fairy would decide to hide Cliff in a book. A book! I can't reach inside books. I might never have known what happened to Cliff if you hadn't had the piece of mirror with you."

"Good job, Prince," I say, scratching behind my dog's

ears. "The mirror wouldn't have broken if not for you!" Prince barks happily, and I turn back to Maryrose. "I tried to bring Cliff home, but I guess he's been in Wonderland so long, he got used to it. And he —" Now his last words to me make sense. "He said as long as I went back, he wouldn't have to. I guess he wanted to make sure I would help you escape. And I will. I will, Maryrose. I promise." I straighten my shoulders. "But will Gluck and his friends come after us again?"

"As you know, Gluck and his friends are powerful," Maryrose says. "They can't enter the real world, but they may try to trap you again. Perhaps in another book. You must promise me you'll be careful."

"I promise," I say. "But, Maryrose, I —"

The mirror ripples and she's gone.

"Wait, Maryrose! I have more questions!" Like why did Gluck and his friends curse her? How long has she been cursed for?

I wait a couple of minutes, but all I see in the mirror is me, Jonah, and Prince.

I have many questions. But no answers. I don't know what shape or form the fairy might try to take next.

But I do know the evil fairy is trying to stop me from helping Maryrose.

Thing is, I WON'T stop trying to free her from the magic mirror.

No matter what.

Back upstairs, Jonah takes Prince into his room, and I head into my room. I spot my jewelry box on my dresser. It's decorated with characters from fairy tales. Whenever I get home from a fairy tale, the characters change to show how the ending of the story changed. But Alice isn't a fairy tale character. And the story changed in Penny's copy of the book.

I head to my bookshelf and take down my copy of *Alice's Adventures in Wonderland*. I flip through the pages. There is no mention of Alice meeting four tiny girls. And no mention of Cliff. So only Penny's copy has changed. Interesting.

I lie down on my bed with the book in my hand.

Is it worth reading, even though I've already kind of lived it? Will it give me a different perspective on what I experienced? Will I learn more about Wonderland? About the people I met? About myself?

Yes, I decide. There's always more to learn. And I turn to page one.

Turn the page for some magical *fun* and games!

Write Your Own Story

One day, you're relaxing on your couch, re-reading your favorite story of all time, when suddenly the book is like a vacuum cleaner and it sucks you inside. AHHHH! What and who do you see?

You're not going to mess the story up. You're not going to mess the story up. You're not going to . . . OOPS. You messed the story up. How did you mess the story up?

You've got to fix the ending! Or maybe you don't?! What do you do?

It's taco night at home and you do NOT want to miss it. How do you get back home?

Word Searches

*Find the Whatever After–themed words:

Abby, Jonah, Maryrose, Penny, Robin, Frankie, Smithville,
Mlynowski, Jax, Gabrielle, ketchup, curse, basement,
spell, magic mirror

```
T  R  O  Z  Y  J  A  X  L  C  F  M  K  P  Y
W  P  R  A  O  O  A  M  P  M  H  W  Y  U  D
G  V  O  Y  L  N  B  A  Q  L  R  S  A  I  D
B  Z  B  D  C  A  B  G  E  Y  P  P  V  Y  U
E  G  I  M  K  H  Y  I  W  N  K  T  H  X  U
Z  P  N  H  E  Z  A  C  Z  O  C  M  J  F  S
S  E  S  N  T  I  X  M  H  W  M  A  L  Q  M
G  N  P  H  C  B  J  I  C  S  L  R  P  Z  I
Z  N  E  I  H  A  F  R  U  K  J  Y  K  O  T
G  Y  L  S  U  S  A  R  L  I  Q  R  C  U  H
G  S  L  F  P  E  Q  O  J  H  Q  O  Z  A  V
K  S  X  O  B  M  M  R  C  U  R  S  E  K  I
G  A  B  R  I  E  L  L  E  H  H  E  F  P  L
Y  Q  U  K  J  N  D  I  H  W  P  Z  Q  P  L
W  S  F  R  H  T  L  X  F  R  A  N  K  I  E
```

229

*Find the *Abby in Wonderland*–themed words:

Wonderland, Alice, Lewis Carroll, Queen of Hearts, Mad Hatter, Gluck, Cheshire, Cliff, tea, tarts, swallow, croquet, golf course, drink me, mushroom

```
P  C  X  R  C  F  C  R  O  Q  U  E  T  A  W
B  Y  E  M  B  Q  Z  W  W  U  T  Y  X  L  O
M  W  N  A  Z  P  W  X  E  E  V  U  S  I  N
U  R  W  D  L  E  X  G  O  E  R  E  Y  C  D
S  P  Y  H  A  M  B  O  V  N  I  C  V  E  E
H  T  G  A  S  W  A  L  L  O  W  H  G  W  R
R  O  D  T  V  R  G  F  M  F  M  E  F  X  L
O  D  R  T  C  T  B  C  X  H  F  S  Z  V  A
O  M  L  E  L  A  P  O  O  E  E  H  Q  N  N
M  I  N  R  I  R  N  U  P  A  A  I  B  O  D
L  P  Y  E  F  T  F  R  O  R  C  R  E  A  A
V  S  C  U  F  S  K  S  E  T  D  E  K  F  B
D  R  I  N  K  M  E  E  O  S  G  L  D  P  T
L  E  W  I  S  C  A  R  R  O  L  L  O  W  E
W  W  S  C  G  L  U  C  K  H  L  U  C  G  A
```

224

Fill in the Blanks

Fill in the Blanks #1

Fill in this list with each type of word to create your own stories:

a. Plural noun _____

b. Noun _____

c. Body part _____

d. Body part _____

e. Article of clothing _____

f. Body part _____

g. Adverb _____

h. Body part (plural) _____

i. Room _____

j. Verb _____

k. Adjective _____

l. Number _____

m. Noun _____

n. Adjective _____

o. Noun (plural) _____

Too Many (o)_____

Thump.

I land facedown on (a)_____. There's a (b)_____
in my (c)_____. Blah. I pick it out and wipe my
(d)_____ on my (e)_____.

"I think I just broke my (f)_____," Jonah mumbles.

"Seriously?" I ask.

"No," Jonah says. "I'm okay."

Good. I'm glad he's okay. Now I don't have to feel bad when I
yell at him. "WHAT WERE YOU THINKING?"

"What do you mean?" he asks (g)_____.

I leap to my feet and tick off the answers on my
(h)_____. "Exhibit A: You drag us to the
(i)_____. Exhibit B: You (j)_____ on the
(k)_____ mirror. And exhibits C, D, and E: You
then proceed to knock (l)_____ *more times* on the
(k)_____ mirror, and when it tries to suck us in? You.
Said. 'COOL!'"

"'Cause it was!" he exclaims. "Come on, Abby! That was
so awesome! That was the most awesomest thing to ever
happen to us."

226

I shake my head. I'm not sure what even happened. Where are we?

I sniff. It smells like (m)_____. I push myself up onto my elbows and look around. I see:

1. (n)_____ (o)_____.

2. More (n)_____ (o)_____.

3. Even MORE (n)_____ (o)_____.

Um, why are there thousands of (n)_____

(o)_____ in my (i)_____?

Wait. My (i)_____ does not have (o)_____.

I turn to Jonah. "We're not in the (i)_____!"

Fill in the Blanks #2

a. Word _____

b. Word that rhymes with the word you chose for (a)

_____

c. Noun _____

d. Game _____

e. Body part _____

f. Room _____

g. Adjective _____

h. Noun _____

i. Body part _____

j. Adjective _____

k. Noun _____

l. Noun _____

m. Adjective _____

n. Sound _____

o. Adjective _____

p. Verb ending in -ing _____

q. Body part (plural) _____

The Evil (e)_____

"I can't believe Aladdin would actually help that guy," Jonah says. "Um, hello! Hasn't he heard the term '(a)_____ (b)_____'?"

Jonah and I watch as the evil (e)_____ studies the kids playing (d)_____, a frown on his (e)_____. He's clearly looking for someone.

Oh. Right.

He's looking for Aladdin. So he can bring Aladdin to the (f)_____ and make him find the (g)_____ (h)_____.

But Aladdin isn't here, because I gave him a (i)_____ bleed.

Oops.

"Um, Jonah?" I say.

"Yeah?" says Jonah.

"I think we — well, I — messed up the story."

Prince wakes up with a bark, as if he's heard me.

Quickly, I explain to Jonah how Aladdin WON'T be able to help the (e)_____ now, due to the bloody (i)_____ I gave him.

"But maybe that's a (j)_____ thing!" Jonah says. "We don't want Aladdin getting mixed up with the evil (e)_____ anyway, right?"

I shake my head. "But Aladdin needs the (k)_____ if he's going to end up with the (l)_____. We have to make this (m)_____!"

(n)_____ (n)_____ (n)_____!

Suddenly, I have an idea. The story never says why the evil (e)_____ picks Aladdin to get the (h)_____.

Maybe it can be any kid.

Maybe it can be . . . us.

"Hey, Jonah," I say. "What if *we* get the (h)_____? Then we'll give it to Aladdin later!"

Jonah looks at me like I'm (o)_____. He does that a LOT. "How?"

"You go up to the evil (e)_____. Start (p)_____ to him. Then he'll take you!"

Jonah's (q)_____ bug out. "Me? You're sending ME over to the evil (e)_____? Have YOU ever heard of (a)_____ (b)_____?"

Fill in the Blanks #3

a. Color _____

b. Color _____

c. Food _____

d. Food _____

e. Food _____

f. Food _____

g. Food _____

h. Body part (plural) _____

i. Adjective _____

j. Evil character _____

k. Verb ending in –ing _____

We Want (d)_____!

Up ahead, through some trees, is a totally adorable cottage.

It's light (a)_____ with a light-(b)_____ roof.

"That's not *our* house," Gretel says. "Our house is half the size

and mud brown." She stares at the cottage. "The doorknob looks

like a (e)_____. I'm so hungry my eyes must be playing

tricks on me."

It does look like a (e)_____. A chocolate-chip

(e)_____. Because it *is* a chocolate-chip

(e)_____. It's the (d)_____ house!

We found it! I bend down and scratch behind my dog's ears.

Good job, Prince!

Jonah lifts his nose and sniffs the air. "Do you smell

(e)_____?" he asks.

"And (f)_____?" Hansel says.

"And (g)_____?" Gretel says.

"Yup, yup, and yup," I say, smiling. "You're all correct. This, my

friends, is the (d)_____ house."

Gretel's (h)_____ almost pop out of her face, slinky

style. "It's real?" she asks.

"Told you so," I say smugly. Take that, Gretel!

Hansel and Gretel start running down the hill. Hansel reaches the house first.

"It smells so (i)_____," Jonah says.

"It does," I say as the (i)_____iest-smelling breeze ever wafts toward me.

"I don't see the (j)_____," Jonah says. "We'll be careful. Let's just take a closer look. We have to. It's a (d)_____ house! It's THE (d)_____ house."

Well . . . we'll have to be careful . . . but . . . if the (j)_____ doesn't see us . . .

My stomach is (k)_____. And I could really use some dessert. And . . . it's the (d)_____ HOUSE! I run down the hill.

A chat with
Whatever After author Sarah Mlynowski
and author Emily Jenkins!

Sarah Mlynowski with her friend and fellow author Emily Jenkins. Which one is the real rabbit and which is the fake one? ☺

Emily: Hi, Sarah.

Sarah: Hi, Emily. Thank you for asking me questions for the back of my book. You're the best.

Emily: Of course. Here we go. You've written eleven books for the Whatever After series so far. Have you always loved fractured fairy tales?

Sarah: Yup. Even as a kid, I loved to twist the original tales. I wrote "Snow White and the Seven Kittens." "Little Blue Riding Hood." "The Princess and the M&M." Because aren't M&Ms so much yummier than peas? Also, all of my stories always ended with the line, "The moral of this story is to never eat crackers in bed." I have no idea why.

Emily: What's your favorite fairy tale and why?

Sarah: My favorite fairy tale is *Cinderella*. I have always wanted to go to a ball. Also the writer in me loves a ticking clock. It's midnight or bust!

Emily: Lewis Carroll, who wrote *Alice's Adventures in Wonderland*, was playing around with famous nursery rhymes, like "The Queen of Hearts, she made some tarts . . ." Did you grow up with nursery rhymes? Tell us one that you like!

Sarah: I used to love "Humpty Dumpty." I would sit up on the tippy-top of the living room couch, call out the Humpty Dumpty rhyme, and tumble onto the cushions at the "had a great fall" part. My parents were not huge fans of the game . . . especially when I taught it to my little sister.

Emily: Who's your favorite *Wonderland* character and why? Mine is the Cheshire Cat.

Sarah: The Mad Hatter. As a kid, I expected him to be uber angry and always yelling at people. I was thrilled to discover that *mad* could also mean *bonkers*. Also, I really liked hats. Sunhats. Baseball hats. Shoe boxes I decorated and wore on my head.

Emily: The Queen of Hearts and her court are a pack of cards. What's your favorite card game and why?

Sarah: Rummy 500. I just taught my eight-year-old daughter how to play. I like a game that you can clean up and then start again a few days later, and it takes us a good week to reach 500. The only problem is when we lose the score sheet. Luckily, my daughter always remembers the score. At least when she's winning.

Emily: Will Jonah ever get into *Jack in the Beanstalk*?

Sarah: Absolutely. Promise! Eventually. Of course, the story will be very, VERY different from what Jonah expects. But before Abby and Jonah meet Jack, they're going to meet a certain princess who's having trouble sleeping . . . look for *Whatever After #11: Two Peas in a Pod* coming next!

Emily: Will the moral of the story be to never eat crackers in bed?

Sarah: No, the moral of the story will be to always check under the mattress for peas. But just for you, I'll throw in something about crackers, too.

Thank you, Emily!

Emily Jenkins is the author of Brave Red, Smart Frog, *a book of fairy tales, as well as the Upside-Down Magic series with Sarah Mlynowski and Lauren Myracle.*

*Word Search Answer Key

```
T  R  O  Z  Y  J  A  X  L  C  F  M  K  P  Y
W  P  R  A  O  O  A  M  P  M  H  W  Y  U  D
G  V  O  Y  L  N  B  A  Q  L  R  S  A  I  D
B  Z  B  D  C  A  B  G  E  Y  P  P  V  Y  U
E  G  I  M  K  H  Y  I  W  N  K  T  H  X  U
Z  P  N  H  E  Z  A  C  Z  O  C  M  J  F  S
S  E  S  N  T  I  X  M  H  W  M  A  L  Q  M
G  N  P  H  C  B  J  I  C  S  L  R  P  Z  I
Z  N  E  I  H  A  F  R  U  K  J  Y  K  O  T
G  Y  L  S  U  S  A  R  L  I  Q  R  C  U  H
G  S  L  F  P  E  Q  O  J  H  Q  O  Z  A  V
K  S  X  O  B  M  M  R  C  U  R  S  E  K  I
G  A  B  R  I  E  L  L  E  H  H  E  F  P  L
Y  Q  U  K  J  N  D  I  H  W  P  Z  Q  P  L
W  S  F  R  H  T  L  X  F  R  A  N  K  I  E
```

* From the Word Search on page 223

*Word Search Answer Key

```
P  C  X  R  C  F (C  R  O  Q  U  E  T) A  W
B  Y  E  M  B  Q  Z  W  W  U  T  Y  X  L  O
M  W  N  A  Z  P  W  X  E  E  V  U  S  I  N
U  R  W  D  L  E  X  G  O  E  R  E  Y  C  D
S  P  Y  H  A  M  B  O  V  N  I  C  V  E  E
H  T  G  A (S  W  A  L  L  O  W) H  G  W  R
R  O  D  T  V  R  G  F  M  F  M  E  F  X  L
O  D  R  T  C  T  B  C  X  H  F  S  Z  V  A
O  M  L  E  L  A  P  O  O  E  E  H  Q  N  N
M  I  N  R  I  R  N  U  P  A  A  I  B  O  D
L  P  Y  E  F  T  F  R  O  R  C  R  E  A  A
V  S  C  U  F  S  K  S  E  T  D  E  K  F  B
(D  R  I  N  K  M  E) E  O  S  G  L  D  P  T
(L  E  W  I  S  C  A  R  R  O  L  L) O  W  E
W  W  S  C (G  L  U  C  K) H  L  U  C  G  A
```

* From the Word Search on page 224

acknowledgments

Thank you, thank you, thank you to:

Everyone at Scholastic, everyone at the Laura Dail Literary Agency, everyone at Deb Shapiro and Company, everyone at Lauren Walters and Co.

Aimee Friedman, Laura Dail, Tamar Rydzinski, Deb Shapiro, Lauren Walters, Olivia Valcarce, Katie Hartman, Lauren Donovan, Jennifer Abbots, Abby McAden, David Levithan, Ellie Berger, Tracy van Straaten, Rachel Feld, Antonio Gonzalez, Robin Hoffman, Sue Flynn, Kerianne Okie, Melissa Schirmer, Lizette Serrano, Emily Heddleson, and everyone in the School Channels and in Sales!

Thank you to all my friends, family, supporters, writing buddies, and first readers:

Targia Alphonse, Tara Altebrando, Bonnie Altro, Elissa Ambrose, Robert Ambrose, Jennifer Barnes, Emily Bender, the Bilermans, Jess Braun, Rose Brock, Jeremy Cammy, Avery Carmichael, the Dalven-Swidlers, Elizabeth Eulberg, the Finkelstein-Mitchells, Stuart Gibbs, Alan Gratz, the Greens, Adele Griffin, Anne Heltzel,

Farrin Jacobs, Emily Jenkins, Lauren Kisilevsky, Maggie Marr, the Mittlemans, Aviva Mlynowski, Larry Mlynowski, Lauren Myracle, Melissa Senate, Courtney Sheinmel, Jennifer E. Smith, the Swidlers, the Steins, Robin Wasserman, Louisa Weiss, the Wolfes, Maryrose Wood, and Sara Zarr.

Extra love and thanks to Chloe, Anabelle, and Todd.

And of course, thank you, Whatever After readers. You are all wonderful.

"Now, I have something important to show everyone. Please follow me."

I am starting to feel uncomfortable. They didn't . . . No. They couldn't have . . . They didn't put the pea under my mattress, did they?

"Can I bring my pancake?" Jonah asks.

Lawrence smiles. "Of course!"

We all stand and follow Lawrence up the stairs — me, Jonah, Minerva, Belly, and Prince.

He's not taking us to our room, is he?

He takes us to our room.

He's not going to point to my bed, is he?

He points to my bed.

"Abby," Lawrence declares, "when you showed up out of the blue last night, seeking shelter from the storm, Minerva and I decided to test you! And you couldn't sleep! Because you felt the pea!"

"What pea?" Jonah asks.

"The one under the very bottom mattress," Minerva says. "I asked Belly to put it there while she was making up your bed last night."

"Belly, be a dear and go up to the top and remove the mattresses one by one," Lawrence says.

This could take a while.

Belly climbs up the ladder. She pushes the top mattress off. Minerva moves that mattress against the wall. Then Belly tosses off the next mattress. Then the next and the next and the next.

A half hour later, only one mattress remains.

Lawrence lifts up the last mattress. "There!"

"What?" I ask, peering over.

"See that?" he asks.

"I don't see anything," Jonah says.

Prince sniffs. He lunges.

"No, Prince!" I say, holding him back.

Because I see it. I see the pea!

It's smushed. But there it is. Right in the center of the bottom of the mattress. It's green and tiny.

I felt that? Under a hundred mattresses? That's why I had so much trouble sleeping?

No way. I had trouble sleeping because I was fifty feet in the air.

"Can Prince eat the pea?" Jonah asks.

"Sure, why not?" Lawrence says. "After all, he's a royal dog!"

"A royal dog?" I repeat, looking from Lawrence to Minerva to Belly.

"Yes! Hurrah!" Lawrence cheers. "You, Abby, are the princess we have been waiting for! You will rule the kingdom of Bog!"

Me?

Princess?

Oh, wow.

I really, really messed up the story this time.

Each time Abby and Jonah get sucked into their magic mirror, they wind up in a different fairy tale — and find new adventures!

Read all the
Whatever After books!

Whatever After #1: FAIREST of ALL

In their first adventure, Abby and Jonah wind up in the story of *Snow White*. But when they stop Snow from eating the poisoned apple, they realize they've messed up the whole story! Can they fix it — and still find Snow her happy ending?

Whatever After #2: IF the SHOE FITS

This time, Abby and Jonah find themselves in Cinderella's story. When Cinderella breaks her foot, the glass slipper won't fit! With a little bit of magic, quick thinking, and luck, can Abby and her brother save the day?

Whatever After #3: SINK or SWIM

Abby and Jonah are pulled into *The Little Mermaid* — a story with an ending that is *not* happy. So Abby and Jonah mess it up on purpose! Can they convince the mermaid to keep her tail before it's too late?

Whatever After #4: DREAM ON

Now Abby and Jonah are lost in Sleeping Beauty's story, along with Abby's friend Robin. Before they know it, Sleeping Beauty is wide awake and Robin is fast asleep. How will Abby and Jonah make things right?

Whatever After #5: BAD HAIR DAY

When Abby and Jonah fall into Rapunzel's story, they mess everything up by giving Rapunzel a haircut! Can they untangle this fairy tale disaster in time?

Whatever After #6: COLD as ICE

When their dog Prince runs through the mirror, Abby and Jonah have no choice but to follow him into the story of the Snow Queen! It's a winter wonderland . . . but the Snow Queen is rather mean, and she FREEZES Prince! Can Abby and Jonah save their dog . . . and themselves?

Whatever After #7: BEAUTY QUEEN

This time, Abby and Jonah fall into the story of *Beauty and the Beast.* When Jonah is the one taken prisoner instead of Beauty, Abby has to find a way to fix this fairy tale . . . before things get pretty ugly!

Whatever After #8: ONCE upon a FROG

When Abby and Jonah fall into the *The Frog Prince,* they realize the princess is so rude they don't even *want* her help! But will they be able to figure out how to turn the frog back into a prince all by themselves?

Whatever After #9: GENIE in a BOTTLE

The mirror has dropped Abby and Jonah into the story of *Aladdin*! But when things go wrong with the genie, the siblings have to escape an enchanted cave, learn to fly a magic carpet, and figure out WHAT to wish for . . . so they can help Aladdin and get back home!

Whatever After #10: SUGAR and SPICE

When Abby and Johah fall into the story of *Hansel and Gretel*, they can't wait to see the witch's cake house (yum). But they didn't count on the witch trapping them there! Can they escape and make it back to home sweet home?

Whatever After #11:
TWO PEAS in a POD

When Abby lands in the story of *The Princess and the Pea*—and has trouble falling asleep on a giant stack of mattresses—everyone in the kingdom thinks SHE is the princess they've all been waiting for. Though Abby loves the royal treatment—can you say unlimited ice cream?—she and Jonah need to find a *real* princess to rule the kingdom . . . *and* find their way back home in time!

Whatever After #12: SEEING RED

My, what big trouble we're in! When Abby and Jonah fall into the story of *Little Red Riding Hood*, they're determined to save Little Red and her grandma from being eaten by the big, bad wolf. But there's quite a surprise in store when the siblings arrive at Little Red's grandma's house.

WHAT HAPPENS WHEN YOUR MAGIC GOES UPSIDE-DOWN?